NeuroNet

NeuroNet

Kristi Casey

TrulyKristi.com

Steven: Thank you for teaching me how to let go.

Lex: Thank you for giving me the space to make my dreams come true.

Noble: Thank you for making things hard. Without the pressure and pain, there'd be no shining diamond.

First Printing, 2024, Truly Kristi, P.O. Box 746, Sautee Nacoochee, GA 30571

If you enjoy this book, please leave a review, share it with others, and recommend it to your local library and book clubs. If you're interested in becoming a creative alchemist like me, subscribe to my free newsletter at TrulyKristi.com. Fall in love with the music and magic of Mayberry Wine at MayberryWine.com. Tag me on social @trulykristi. And keep shining.

Thank you for being a reader, my friend. The world needs more people like you.

it for work, or if she always keeps it on, but a red light blinks and she's now live in front of five million viewers plus the seventy million who might watch it on-demand.

The reporter smiles brilliantly. "This is Roz Able from *Humanity Now*. I'm with NeuroNet co-founder Dr. Teagan McKenna. Good morning, Dr. McKenna."

Teagan tries to keep her smile from turning into a grimace as she returns the pleasantry. Roz's lips didn't stick to her teeth. Teagan makes a mental note to ask what her secret is later.

Roz lowers her head to signal her seriousness. "As you know, one of your Model Two androids was hit by a train at the Civic Center MARTA station this morning. How common is it for NeuroNet bots to malfunction in this way?"

Teagan is grateful for the softball question. "First, Roz, I'd like to point out that we're not certain if there was a malfunction. I'll need to review the video of the incident and examine dashboard data from this companion before we can say conclusively what did occur. But I can tell you that fewer than one percent of NeuroNet's uploaded population require any kind of repair."

"Fewer than one percent?" Roz looks incredulous.

Teagan nods. She's not done with this interview yet, but it feels like it's going well. "Yes. Fewer than one percent. That's not something you can say about any other technology."

Roz cocks her head. "Some people are calling this a suicide. How would you respond to that?"

Teagan resists the urge to smile. Roz has teed up her sound bite perfectly. "Why would someone who was saved from death want to take their own life?"

That is the button Roz needs. She wraps up the interview. The feed goes dark momentarily as Roz's image is replaced by Ascha's. The PR director gives Teagan a long, slow ovation. "Well done."

Teagan rushes to the table and greedily gulps down water. She spills some down her front, but it will dry in the car. "Thanks. I'll let you

From the Executive Suite's deck, Teagan feels on top of the world. "I never get tired of this view." It makes her grateful to be alive. She takes Carter's hand and squeezes it. "When things feel overwhelming, I like to remind myself: we built this."

He chuckles. "This city was here for hundreds of years before us."

She punches his shoulder. "You know what I mean."

He rubs his arm. "I know." He points toward a dingy side street on the edge of Home Park. "It's hard to believe that twenty years ago we were prototyping the upload Net system on Stinky's Pub napkins down there. Can you believe fifteen years ago we launched the Model Ones . . . ?"

Teagan thinks about how good it felt to secure that round of funding. She felt flush enough to propose to Em. Carter and Melody got engaged. They all married soon after. "Where did the time go?"

She feels Carter's mood shift, and she knows what he's thinking before he says it: "Why does the bad shit always have to happen on a beautiful day?"

"It's a Tuesday, too," she adds. Beautiful Tuesdays have been particularly unkind to them. Carter lost his mother and his wife on days like this.

"Oh . . . fuck you, Tuesday." He shakes a fist at the uncaring gods.

She sees old hurts bubbling up inside her friend. She pulls him into a hug. They take a moment. There is solace in that simple act of holding.

They've been each other's support system since middle school when Carter's family moved to Atlanta. They arrived at the beginning of their seventh-grade year. His father was running away from New York and the life they'd had before 9/11. Trying to forget that his wife's body might never be dug out of the rubble. Hiding from the burden of being a single parent to his pre-teen son. Buried in guilt and grief, Carter's father never really recovered. Alcohol offered an escape without relief, and that left Carter to raise himself. That's how he became a de facto member of Teagan's family. With Em, they became the Three Geeky Musketeers of Central High. He was her favorite lab partner and constant companion through their undergrad and grad school days at Tech. Working together made NeuroNet feel less like a labor of love and more like a family business.

Teagan thinks of Carter's family. Twelve years ago, on a Tuesday like this, they got the call about Melody's car accident. *Too late. We couldn't save her.* Only the child, Rhys, was salvageable.

Teagan doesn't know if she believes in God. But if one or many exist, they must have a cruel sense of humor: to take Carter's beloved spouse and leave the one she'd gladly give away. She pats Carter on the back and releases him. It's time to get to work and figure out what they're dealing with. He smiles. She notices his face is getting puffy. Something about the cheeks and eyes reminds her of his father. *Is it grief?*

"You look rough," she says, reluctantly heading toward the Executive Suite's entrance.

Carter scratches the back of his neck and flashes a lopsided grin. "I haven't been sleeping well."

Teagan laughs and sticks her thumb in the biometric lock. The door slides open with a soft whoosh. "I'm glad I slept like a rock last night. I have a feeling we're all going to lose a lot of sleep over . . . whatever this is."

She drops her purse on a fluffy white couch she and Carter bought on a whim. It looks like a marshmallow had a baby with a cloud. When they purchased it, they intended it to be a spot to 'chill-out.' Teagan smiles wryly. She can't remember the last time they used it.

Carter swings past to tilt the screens around his desk toward her. "Do you need a minute to get coffee or go to the bathroom first?"

"No. Brief me." Teagan leans against the edge of her desk. "What are we dealing with?"

Carter points to a screen with NeuroNet dashboard data on it. "The bot's name was Dee Claybourne. Originally uploaded to an Eye with Model One tech and was one of the first companions to get a synthetic body after we launched the Model Two upgrade ten years ago."

Teagan whistles. "An O.G."

"It would save us a lot of bad press," Teagan says, doing a quick scan of new messages. "No one's sent me anything useful. Is Tito ready for us to come down?"

Carter shakes his head. "Not yet. He's analyzing the cognitive data from Dee's last few days, looking for any patterns or anomalies. He wants us down in the lab after lunch."

"Shit." Teagan pinches the bridge of her nose.

Carter's brow creases in concern. "What is it?"

"Em's coming in for a fitting this afternoon. Think we can squeeze her in during a break?"

Carter's mouth falls open. Teagan holds up a warning finger. "Don't say it."

He feigns innocence. "What?"

She folds her arms and waits.

Carter busies himself with his wall of screens, pivoting them back to face his chair. He turns to say something.

She shakes her head and warns, "Don't do it."

A half-smile creeps up his face. She leans forward to hiss, "You are such an asshole."

His face ripples with surprise. "What? I didn't say anything."

Teagan glares at him. "You didn't have to."

He shrugs. That smile is back. "I mean, if you're going to—"

She balls up her fists. "I swear to God, Carter, I will throttle you."

He holds up a shh-ing finger and points to the Eye. "Don't want them to hear you say that. What if something happens to me? You'd be their number one suspect."

"Oh no I won't," Teagan laughs. "I'm one of thousands who'd love to kill you."

He holds his hands over his heart. "Ouch!"

She smiles. "But, if it makes you feel any better, I'd be the only one who'd miss you."

"That does not." Carter's mouth twists to hide a smile. "But you know would make me feel a whole lot better?"

Teagan is suspicious. "What?"

"Reminding you—"

"—don't say it—"

He can't hold back the smile anymore. "I told you so."

"Ugh!" Teagan throws her stapler at him. He dodges it easily, but she meant to miss him.

He wags a finger at her. "Rude!" But he can't resist rubbing it in. "I knew you'd cave in."

She leans back. "I didn't cave in. Em's coming in for a fitting. No one said she's getting a body."

Mischief lights up his eyes. "Oh, that's cruel."

Teagan tsks. "I'm just kidding."

"No, you're not!" Carter is no longer a fan of Em. "But how funny would that be? Or mercy, really? She'll think she's going to be uploaded, but we just drag our feet until she kicks it. That's brilliant, Teagan. Cruel, but brilliant."

Teagan grimaces. "That's your idea of funny? That's dark."

He tilts his head and smirks. "C'mon, there's a part of you that wants to laugh."

He's right, but Teagan shakes her head. "You're terrible!"

He holds up his hands. "Am I though? I mean, wouldn't you rather be free?"

"What's free? I've been married too long. What would I do with freedom?"

He sits on the edge of his desk. "Oh, it'd be fun, being single together again. I could be your wingman. You could take me to My Sister's Room . . ."

Teagan cackles. "I'm too old for that lesbian bar now. I'm afraid it'd be more like, 'My Granddaughter's Room.' Besides, no one wants to see a straight cis man in their safe queer space."

"We could double date then! Do adult things, like restaurants . . ."

Teagan shakes her head and sighs with exasperation. "I already do restaurants with you. It's not like Em keeps me locked in the house."

NeuroNet wasn't the only company founded to extract memories and digitally preserve them. They weren't even the first ones to successfully upload human consciousness. But Teagan's design, with its clusters of neural networks operated by Carter's gated AI system, was the first able to consistently mirror how the human brain worked and faithfully reproduce human-like responses. Within the first five years, NeuroNet buried the competition. The Model Two launch catapulted them beyond the reach of the copycats. Now, instead of hospice care, the well-to-do from all over the world seek out their services to keep their families together before loved ones pass.

"Do you remember why we do this?" Teagan asks.

Tito cocks his head. "So, you never have to say goodbye to the ones you love?"

"We've failed at our mission." Teagan closes what's left of Dee's eyes. "Someone who loved Dee had to say goodbye to her for good this time."

"Technically, we could download her into a new body," Tito points out. "I've got her original source files stored on the NeuroNet."

Carter interjects. "No. Not yet. We don't know what prompted this. If we download the same data set we may get the same result. We can't risk another loved one self-destructing. I've been on the phone all morning with the investors."

Teagan notices a vein in his forehead beginning to throb. "How close are we to this round's fundraising goal?"

"Only sixty percent," Carter moans. "I'm already behind pace and three of the biggest fish are threatening to pull out."

Teagan feels sick. If he can't turn things around, this will be the third straight year NeuroNet shows a loss. Everyone knows investing in research and development is crucial for tech survival, but no one wants to fund it. There's no way their sales—impressive as they are—can cover operating and R&D expenses. Before the tech bubble burst twenty years ago, companies like Tesla could lose money hand over fist and still trade with insane valuations. Not anymore. NeuroNet must show a profit this year. And Teagan's determined they will—even if it's only a profit of one dollar. She clears her throat. "Do you want me to ask Aya for help?"

Tito perks up at the name of his former work wife. Dr. Aya Wakahisa, the fourth NeuroNet co-founder, designed the upload process and its machinery while Tito tooled around with different containers to house human consciousness. She cashed out her founder's shares and walked twelve years ago. But before that, Tito and Aya worked side by side on the interface that tied AI-controlled content to container and became devoted companions in the process. He smiles. "That's a great idea."

Carter flushes a deep crimson. "No. It's not."

"Oh, come on, Carter, she's got the money," Tito says.

"I don't want her help." Carter stares them both down. "Ever."

Teagan can tell by his tone of voice that it's time to change the subject. "What did you discover from the dashboard data, Tito?"

Tito's magic eyebrows release the glasses, and they crash back onto his nose. He pivots a workstation screen so Teagan can see. "Cognitive spikes, but not where I expected to see them."

Teagan and Carter step closer. She's used to parsing data from read-outs. Whenever there's an issue with a bot it's the first thing they look at. And the Eye alerts them if there are any units in distress, like last year, when one family took their companion whitewater rafting and the loved one was thrown out of the boat. The cognitive spikes from that accident set off alarms all over the lab. Teagan expects Dee's dashboard data to have several spikes: at the moment of impact, with some smaller peaks prior, indicating either surprise at being pushed or distress, if she jumped.

Instead, the line indicating cognitive irregularities is flat right up until it ends. *That's not normal.* Teagan shrinks the chart until she finds a peak and then zooms into the timeline again. She checks the date. It doesn't make sense. "Three days ago? That was the last time there was a spike? Did you corroborate this with the family?" Tito nods. "What happened three days ago?"

4

Tito leads Teagan and Em past the upload bays toward the warren of fitting rooms. There, in a chamber with smooth, ivory-colored walls, in front of a wooden egg-shaped pod, he begins his client-facing spiel.

Teagan appreciates his professionalism, but Em's eyes glaze over. She gives Em's hand three quick squeezes: a quiet 'I love you.' Em returns the gesture without glancing her way and Teagan feels better. When she sees the pod, however, her lips curl. *Em's going to hate being in there.* Teagan didn't enjoy her three minutes in it and she's not claustrophobic. Em is.

She remembers the unpleasant feeling of warm saline gel encasing her from when she was fit for a body. *Like being harassed by an alien.* Although she's not sure if it would have been any better had the gel been cold. *Creepy feeling either way.*

She'd tried to get out of having a shell for herself made, but Carter wouldn't let her. "Imagine how cool it would be," Carter had said, "for you and an android version of yourself to walk out on stage together. It'd be the perfect way to announce the NeuroNet Model Twos!"

"And show how Model Two skins can look exactly like their loved one!" Tito's face had lit up. "The investors would eat it up. Totally skux!"

Carter had jumped on his support and kept pushing. "Teagan, it'd be a powerful illustration of how far our technology has come and why we're worthy of greater investment. Imagine how excited people will be to transfer loved ones out of their household Eyes and into real-looking bodies. Android shells that look like their beloved!"

Teagan had fought them both. She didn't want to be measured for a body. She hated the idea of replicating herself. It was creepy imagining a robotic version of her body might be stored in the Meat Locker after the party. The whole thing smacked of two-bit carnival showmanship.

"Aren't we better than this?" she had asked. But without Aya there to support her, it was two against one. She eventually gave in to the boys.

And they were right. The stunt generated the perfect amount of excitement, buzz, and pre-orders that NeuroNet needed to grow. Looking back, Teagan sees that giving loved ones synthetic bodies was the tipping point that enabled the company to expand globally. Teagan is proud of that.

What she isn't proud of is the supplementary revenue stream that dummy version spawned: an AI-only line of Model Two companions meant for pleasure, not companionship. Teagan is embarrassed that this line of sexbots is NeuroNet's most lucrative division. *Because why would a man upload his wife when he could order an eternally youthful girlfriend with no memory or baggage?* And yes, user data had proved her right. The empty-headed line appealed mostly to men. She could count the number of female customers for that division on two hands. For a while, the child-size AI-only models were popular with grief-stricken parents. But that appeal wore thin when people realized they'd need to replace the units every couple of years if they wanted the child to 'grow' with them. Now, they're purchased only by brothels. As much as Teagan finds the idea distasteful, she's grateful that they're replacing real children in the sex trade.

She hears Em ask, "Can you fill out my curves a little? I've lost my ass with all the chemo." And it makes Teagan laugh. *It's not good enough that you get your chance at eternal life, you need something else.*

Tito chuckles and shakes his head. "No, I'm sorry. We don't enhance the companion's body. The pod takes exact measurements, and we manufacture the shell based off those dimensions."

"You can't even give me straight hair?"

"Thanks, Teagan," Tito says. "Good luck."

"I won't need it," Teagan lies. She lifts the edge of the changing room curtain. "How are you doing?"

"You can come in," Em replies with a laugh. "You've seen me naked before."

"I didn't want to assume." Teagan pushes the curtain aside. Em undresses slowly; her fingers linger over her edges, as if comforting the flesh. Teagan is gripped with a desire to embrace her, kiss her neck. She wants to grab her hips and pull Em close. Take her on the rug of this space. It's a hot thought. Teagan knows there aren't cameras in the dressing room, but the noises they make would be picked up by the Eye in the pod room. *No, thank you.* She's sure Carter and Tito would be impressed by her chutzpa, but they'd also tease her for weeks.

Instead of jumping her wife, Teagan gathers the clothes Em has deposited on the floor, folds them, and places them on the shelf designated for personal items. She catches a glimpse of Em putting on her robe in the mirror. Em's bones move like knitting needles under the skin. "You've gotten so thin."

Em ties the robe's sash. "And I thought you liked me bony." She grabs a jutting hip bone. "That's okay. I miss having an ass, too."

Teagan feels guilty. *She really looks like she's dying.*

Em frowns at the mirror. "Too bad you can't fill out my curves a little when you make me a new body. I have enough things wrong with my head, I don't want people to think I'm anorexic, too."

"They won't," Teagan assures her. "They'll probably think you look like a model."

"That's terrible," Em says. And then she laughs.

Teagan is thankful Em is in a better mood now than when she arrived. She kisses Em's cheek. "It's a slippery slope. Believe me, more than a few people have tried to bribe us to 'enhance' their loved ones. But waking up in a synthetic body is difficult enough. Inhabiting one that is different from the one you remember could create cognitive dissonance. And dissonance causes accidents. Accidents like Dee. It's too risky."

"I don't know." Em is in the bathroom. "Seems like most people wish they were someone else. Might be nice to get a second chance to be different after death." She reads the list of required fluids. "Saliva, mucus, tears, vaginal fluid, urine, and feces?" She raises her eyebrows. "I've got to leave samples of all of these?"

"I can help you if you want."

Em waves her off. "The last thing I want is for my wife to swab my ass. Why do you need all this?"

"It's not just your body that we replicate. We match the consistency, odor, and taste of the fluids. Well, most of them. Some we adapt a little."

Em's eyebrows shoot up. "You mean I'm still going to have to deal with boogers even after I'm uploaded?"

"The fluid reserves are primarily for the guardians," Teagan says. "It makes living with an android less awkward. And it also helps your transition out of a human body into a mechanical one if, when a sad memory is triggered, you can cry and get stuffed up. Those kinds of things help you appear and feel more human." Em does not look convinced. Teagan adds, "Fluids consistent with ones you excrete while alive also help with arousal and— "

Em smirks. "It makes sex with a robot less awkward."

Teagan blushes. "Yes."

"Still . . . how many robots piss and shit?"

"Your shell is powered by biomass. You eat and drink to fuel up. And what's a more lifelike way to eliminate the waste byproducts? It's an elegant solution, but we make it more hygienic. The biomass waste doesn't smell bad and it's non-toxic. It helps preserve the illusion of life, for you and others."

Em wrinkles her nose. "Seems like non-odiferous pee would take all the fun out of golden showers."

Teagan laughs. "Would you rather I plug you into the wall at night? That was the first engineering solution we tried. I could always install a human-size charging station in the walk-in closet."

"That's just creepy." Em shivers and pulls on a robe. "No, thank you. I don't want to live in a closet like a vampire."

"Biomass puts you in control of your energy levels, so you don't have to worry about conking out if I forget to charge you. Having familiar activities like eating, drinking, and using the bathroom also should make your transition easier. And allow you to participate in social gatherings without standing out."

Em looks at the sample jars. "Are you going to make me have my period, too?"

"No. Cancer treatments kicked you into early menopause, so there's no need. It wouldn't be what you'd experience in life."

Em raises both fists and pumps them. "Yay!"

"Yay, menopause!" Teagan echoes. She's having fun. "There will be synthetic blood pockets under your new skin, but it's purely cosmetic, in case you get a scrape. You won't be filled with blood like you are now. After your procedure, I'll keep a special vial of repair serum so if you scratch or tear the skin, I can fix it myself."

Em nods and her hand brushes her robe, exposing a network of tidy white scars crisscrossing her upper thigh. Teagan debates not saying anything. But she can't help it. She must add, "If you cut yourself, we'll have to come in and get you patched up. I can't fix self-harm at home."

Em scowls. "Why did you bring that up?"

Why did I? Is that a risk factor? Did Dee self-harm? Self-harm isn't always an indicator that someone is suicidal. But they're at greater risk of attempting it than the general population. *Is it possible that Dee was suicidal before being uploaded? Could this morning's accident be a suicide? If so, would an uploaded Em choose a similar action?* Teagan runs her fingers over the scars on Em's thigh. "You didn't have these when we got married."

Em pulls away and closes the bathroom door. "I don't do that anymore," she calls out. She sounds hurt. "I'm surprised you even noticed."

"Why wouldn't I notice?"

Em doesn't respond.

But I didn't notice . . . Teagan fingers a circular piece of jade at her neck with four curved arms. It's a gift from Tito. Something his grandfather used to catch birds when he was a boy in New Zealand. Feeling its edges calms her. It's warm, like her skin. And familiar. She strokes it, waiting for Em to reemerge.

When Em finally does, she fixes Teagan with a sad look. "I don't know why you gave consent."

"Why? Because I love you." *I do.*

"You don't hate me and want me to die?" She sounds so childish and hurt.

"No. Of course not." Teagan gives Em a little shake. "Sometimes I don't like you. But I would never wish that on you. I love you."

Em relents. She throws her arms around Teagan's neck and says, "If you love me, promise me something."

Teagan sighs, relieved. "Anything."

"Promise me you won't work so hard. That you'll spend more time with me. Once I'm uploaded, take two weeks off. Let's have a honeymoon and start over again. We don't have to go anywhere; we can stay at home. I just want you all to myself. Can you do that?"

Teagan winces. "I don't know if I can promise that. We've got this issue with Dee, and they need me here until we've resolved it. Plus, we're gearing up for our initial public offering. Carter's raising funds and he might need my help."

Em's face hardens. "Whom do you love more: me or Carter?"

Teagan can't answer that without sounding like an asshole. "That's a ridiculous question. You know I'd love to go away with you. But I have obligations that keep me here."

"When was the last time you took a vacation?"

"I can't remember."

Em sticks a bony finger in Teagan's chest. "See? You're due."

"I'm not an employee with PTO time. I'm a founder. We don't get time off. Who's left to mind the shop if I piss off?"

"What about a staycation? Just don't go in, but still be here if they need you. Can you give me that?"

Teagan takes Em's hands in hers. She's not sure how that would work, but she tries to sound sincere. "I'll figure out a way to make it happen."

It's enough for Em. She smiles. "Good."

"You ready?"

Em nods. Teagan takes her hand and leads her to the pod.

Em pulls the breathing tube out of its wrapper. "Will you help me with this?"

"Of course." Teagan takes it from her hands. As she does, Em kisses her. The girlish gesture catches Teagan off-guard. She pulls back and smiles. *After everything, she still churns me up with her kisses.* "What was that for?"

Em throws her arms around Teagan's neck. "For good luck, pod captain. You're going to need it to keep me from freaking and drowning out in there."

"I'll be right here." Teagan assures her with a kiss. "You'll be fine. Just imagine you're floating in the ocean. You like open sea."

"I do." Em nuzzles Teagan's neck.

Teagan sighs. *We can make this work.* She kisses Em, lingering on her sweet lips. Then she gently extracts herself to take up the mouthpiece packet. As she unfurls it, she says, "Teeth together and lips apart."

Em complies.

Teagan smooths the petals of the breathing apparatus against Em's teeth. She presses Em's lips against them to create a seal. Em tries to say something.

"Don't speak," Teagan warns. "Just breathe through your mouth."

Em nods.

Teagan kisses Em's forehead. It feels clammy. "I'm nervous, too," Teagan admits.

Em tries to smile.

"Don't, or you'll break the seal." The smile vanishes. Teagan squeezes Em's hand. *I love you.* "Remember: don't move. Breathe through your mouth and keep your eyes closed. I'll be right here. Press the button when you're ready to begin."

Em nods and disrobes, handing the garment to Teagan. Em lays down on the plank, bones grinding against the skin in a way that Teagan finds alarming.

"Does it hurt, laying on the plank like that?"

Em shakes her head. Teagan helps her plug the oxygen pipeline into the ceiling, and kisses her head. "You're going to be safe. Just relax. I'm looking after you." She backs out.

As Em presses the button to close the hatch, Teagan shudders, remembering how the gel rushed in over her naked body. "Remember to close your eyes! Focus on your breath when it gets to your neck. You're going to do fine. Don't panic!"

Em flashes a thumbs-up as the door shuts. Teagan peers through the circular pod window. She sees many Ems, as if she is looking into a spider's multifaceted eye. She blows a kiss, but isn't sure Em gets it. *Hopefully, she can feel it. What the hell, she'll be fine. I'm the one freaking out.* Teagan strokes the robe in her arms, finding consolation in its smooth satin weave. Woven of the most luxurious cotton, it is the best robe money can buy. She knows because she chose it for the fitting rooms. It is supposed to reinforce the idea that uploading a dying loved one to the NeuroNet is the best choice.

The pod hums. Teagan shudders. *Soon, I'll no longer be a wife, I'll be a guardian.* The thought occupies an uncomfortable space. Being married is a restriction that sometimes chafes her. Guardianship will impose new restrictions on her life. She rubs her wrist. She doesn't wear a watch or bracelets. She hates the feel of them. But she'll need to get used to it. All guardians are issued a biometric wristlet so NeuroNet can track their vital signs—just in case.

It's a government safety requirement for all guardians. And all NeuroNet companions and sexbots need to be registered with the local police jurisdiction. Teagan and the boys fought the regulations in court. And lost. Their lawyers argued it was a violation of privacy. But the government's lawyers argued that anything AI-enabled—even gated like the NeuroNet interface is—needed direct human supervision. Teagan agrees that bots need supervision, but she doesn't like that NeuroNet monitors the vitals of the guardians, too. *As if companions are monsters who might inflict harm. They're people someone loved too much to let die.*

But there are practical benefits. It's good to know when a guardian dies, so the loved one can be deactivated. Not having bots walk around unsupervised is one thing Teagan and the U.S. government agree on.

The pod must be filled with gel already. Teagan can hear the hum of the ultrasound device measuring Em's body. *Have any customers changed their mind after getting the measurements done?* She can't think of any. The law puts special emphasis on consent. Both spouses must agree to upload. Family members can request guardianship of a minor or a single relative. But the marriage rite's 'till death do us part' can't be overruled unless both halves of the couple are on board.

But some of them must have at least thought about backing out, or we'd never see companion divorces. And that is a thing now. Only when a divorce between guardian and loved one is awarded, there's only one beneficiary.

Teagan thinks those kinds of divorces must be more satisfying than normal ones. *You don't have to give your ex anything, and you get to deactivate them. That's got to be the best 'fuck you.'*

5

Teagan enters the Executive Suite. The first thing she notices is the docked Eye. Carter's workstation is booted up. He's typing in queries.

"Working on something sensitive?" The Eyes are government-issue. Every office and household has at least one. But you have the right to dock the assistant for privacy or if you are working on something involving intellectual property, trade secrets or the like.

Carter gestures her over. Even when the Eye is off he doesn't trust that it's not listening. He tilts his screen toward her and scribbles a note on a pad he keeps by his elbow: *Dee's medical history.*

She writes back: *Why?*

Just in case we need it.

Teagan frowns. *Find anything interesting?*

Carter shrugs. *Bipolar disorder.*

Teagan's stomach twists. *Em's bipolar.*

Inconclusive connection. Don't worry. Carter smiles. "Unless you want to use that as an excuse to get out of uploading her."

Teagan punches his shoulder. "Not funny."

He laughs anyway.

Teagan glances at the Eye. Nothing blinks or whirrs, but she doesn't trust it. Technically, what Carter is doing is not a legitimate reason to enact blackout protocol. He's violating medical privacy laws. If that comes to light, it will get them into trouble.

She boots up her workstation, knowing it will reactivate the Eye. *Time to get off the dark webs and back to business.*

Carter's always been a hacker. It's always been risky. But now, they have something significant they could lose. She doesn't know why he persists in doing it. *We're almost fifty, for Chrissakes.*

Carter shuts down his workstation. "How did Em handle the fitting?"

"Surprisingly well. She was nervous. But it's something she really wants."

Thankfully, he doesn't ask if it's what Teagan wants. Instead, he says, "Do you want to get dinner tonight?"

"I can't."

He nods. "Have to rush home? It was a big day. Em will be glad to see you."

Teagan flushes. "Actually, I've got a . . . thing on the Westside."

Carter perks up. "Anything I'd like?"

He must be lonely and looking for a distraction. *This is awkward.* Teagan debates lying, but reasons he would be hurt worse if she does. She admits, "No. It's a reception with Aya for Kakumei. They're launching a new product line called Neural Nirvana."

The tips of Carter's ears turn pink. "Why would you go to a Kakumei party with Aya?"

"We're still friends."

"So go out for drinks." Carter scowls. "You're really going to her company's event? Why?"

Why does he have to be so petty? "Because I'm one of her biggest investors."

He just stares, looking hurt.

Teagan pushes her screens out of the way to give him her full attention. "I know you and Aya have your differences, but she's brilliant. And I think what she's doing is innovative."

"It's pseudoscience."

There's no way she can win this argument without putting his nose out of joint. Aya's been telling the media that Neural Nirvana helps people modify their behavior and become better versions of themselves.

Carter thinks anything mental health-related that isn't connected to therapy is pseudoscience.

But Aya isn't a wellbeing influencer; she's a gifted neurobiologist with serious engineering skills. The way she was able to map the way the brain operates so Teagan could hard-code the NeuroNet . . . Teagan will never stop fangirling. If Aya says she's discovered a way to electro stimulate the brain to break unhealthy habits, Teagan knows that's exactly what she's done. She shrugs at Carter. "Well, I'm excited to see how Kakumei's new headdresses work. Want me to save you a seat?"

"No, thank you," Carter says. A smirk creeps across his lips. "But when the first lawsuits get filed in five years and Kakumei implodes, you can buy me popcorn."

The Eye flashes before Teagan can respond. "Incoming call from Dr. Tito Ngata." Carter accepts the call. Tito's chiseled head and torso appear in effigy in-between their desks.

"You need to see this," Tito says. The screens fill with grainy security footage. A woman of middle age enters the field of view. "That's Dee, this morning." She stops only to let people pass by. She slowly and deliberately walks to the subway platform's edge. The lights of a train approach. A man passes behind her. It looks like she's about to step out into the train's path. The feed goes dark.

"That's it?" Teagan rewinds the footage and plays it again. "Where's the rest of it?"

"That's all we have," Tito says. "Cops confirm they're not holding onto anything else. This is all their investigation has, too."

Teagan frowns. "It looks like she was about to jump."

"I don't think so." Carter leans back and folds his arms over his chest. "The man who passed behind her could have pushed her."

Tito pushes his glasses up. "There have been several subway attacks recently."

"I don't like how close to the edge she moved," Teagan says. "It looked like she was about to do something."

Carter laughs. "Don't be ridiculous. She was probably trying to get a view of the train, to see if it was coming."

NeuroNet androids do follow behavioral patterns formed when they were alive. But something about the way Dee walked to the platform seemed determined. "She wasn't moving casually," Teagan says.

"You think she intended to commit suicide?" Carter's face hardens.

"I'm not saying that." Teagan looks to Tito for help. "But, we can't deny it's in the realm of possibility. I don't think we have enough evidence to write it off."

6

Teagan's car hurtles toward the Westside. It's pushing the government speed limit, but Teagan wishes it could go faster. She hates being late. The Neural Nirvana launch party started an hour ago. She isn't even halfway there.

You're just pissed because you want alone time with Aya. And now you're afraid she'll be too busy for you. But it's not like you had a date. And this is her event. You'll be lucky to get five minutes, no matter when you arrive. Besides, Aya would understand why you couldn't leave earlier.

Dee Claybourne's dashboard had presented the NeuroNet team with Teagan's least favorite combination: too much data and too little to go on. She, Carter, and Tito had to comb through everything and then decide on what updates they could communicate. Before leaving, she had to go over potential media narratives with Ascha. *And the day's not over yet. I still need to approve the statement when Ascha's done.* She watches raindrops splatter, bead, and slide off the windshield. For the first time in hours, she thinks of Em. *Oh shit, I need to check in!*

She tells the car's console to make the call. Em's LED-enhanced image smiles. "Are you on your way?"

"No," Teagan says, "I have a work thing."

"A work thing?" The smile vanishes. "That you're leaving for now?" The double crease between Em's brow that she calls 'Teagan lines' appear. "It's half past eight."

"I know, but Ascha needed media advisories, board, and investor statements to send off in the morning. And before we could discuss which angle to take, we had to analyze all the data from Dee's original upload date to present day."

Em's expression does not change. "The Eye could have spit out an analysis in seconds."

"You know how buggy AI can be," Teagan says. "And if it doesn't know, it makes things up that sounds true. Sometimes it's faster to just do it yourself."

Em's Teagan lines deepen. "Where are you going? Is it important?"

To me. It's important to me, Teagan thinks, but that's never held much weight with Em. "It's the Neural Nirvana launch party, Dr. Wakahisa's new project."

"You mean Aya." Em clenches her jaw. "You're going to see Aya instead of coming home?"

"It's not what you think." Teagan can hear the fight coming. "I have to go."

Em likes to use Teagan's crush on Aya as a bargaining chip. When Em's feeling generous, Aya is a reason why they should open their relationship. When Em's jealous, Aya is why Teagan doesn't love her anymore. It's maddening. *You can have chemistry without cheating. Aya and I have only ever been friends.*

Teagan attempts to diffuse the tension. "A launch party is a huge deal. Aya's an old friend. I need to be there for moral support. Remember how terrified I was when we launched the Model Twos? Aya showed up for me . . . and that was after she'd quit NeuroNet."

Em drops her arms and pouts. "I don't feel well. What time will you be home?"

Teagan doesn't trust Em when she gives in so fast. It means there are strings attached. She doesn't look forward to discovering what they are, but she is glad to avoid the fight. "I'll try to be home by ten."

"Can you make it nine?"

"Only if I leave as soon as I get there." *Please,* she begs with her eyes. *I've looked forward to this event for weeks. And I really need Aya's perspective on what happened to Dee.*

"Fine," Em says. "But I'll remember you chose Aya over me." She ends the call before Teagan can respond.

Teagan considers calling her back. But then thinks: *why should I? I'm not doing anything wrong.* Besides, the car has arrived.

The car touches down in front of a trendy, repurposed industrial space that used to be a slaughterhouse. Fifty years ago, no one came here but heroin addicts and hookers. Teagan notes with irony the streets bustle with a new type of hustler, the legal kind: tech luminaries and influential personalities.

Teagan enables the car's valet protocol and hands it over to a young woman with body mods. The club's doors swing open as Teagan approaches. She looks for the motion tracker and smiles when she spots its tell-tale red glow. *Sometimes old tech is the best.*

The doors close behind her. A rhythmic pulse trickles down from the far end of the corridor, but she is alone in the long, candle-lit hallway. She walks towards the sound of water flowing over rocks. Teagan chuckles. *Aya knows how to provoke a mood.* What is it she used to say? *How you do one thing is how you do everything.* Aya never does things in half-measures. Teagan is glad she didn't bail on coming. *This will be something.*

A service Eye hovers up with a tray of drinks glimmering like liquid jewels. She chooses a pink one with a large flower garnish. It is delicious but lacks alcohol. Teagan tries not to look annoyed. She could use a little social lubricant. *I'll bet Aya doesn't want anyone's senses dulled before she reveals her brilliance.*

The low murmur of people talking rises above the sound of gurgling water. Teagan takes another sip, hoping the drink at least has some kind of mood-altering or calming property. She always feels awkward in crowds, and being with Aya doubles her social anxiety.

At the end of the hallway, she finds a waterfall with an interactive menu of options projected against it. Teagan reaches towards a green option labeled 'Life.' A vine-covered stairway emerges. She hits the back button and selects the yellow 'Clarity' option. A golden ramp appears.

A voice from behind her says, "You have always been such a dilettante. Why not trust your first impulse?" Teagan jumps, spilling her drink.

"I do." Teagan rubs liquid from the front of her blouse and tries to hide the puddle she's made on the floor with her foot. "Has it occurred to you that I like to see all the options before committing to any one?"

"Of course." Aya smiles and Teagan's stomach flips. "I think of everything."

Teagan flashes what she hopes is a winning smile. "I'm not sure what I'm about to experience, but I suspect it's going to be amazing."

"It will be." Aya's face radiates joy and calm. She burns so brightly that she sucks all the oxygen out of the room.

Teagan feels breathless. "How is it that you never age? It's been a dozen years, yet you look the same."

"You do, too," Aya says, cocking her head and looking Teagan over. "Maybe a little fuller in the hips."

Teagan laughs, disheartened. "You mean I've grown fat."

"No." Aya smiles. "I mean, I like the way you have filled out. It suits you. We have become the women we were always meant to be." Aya squeezes her hand. "I am so glad you came."

And just like that, Teagan feels better about being thick.

"I want to show you something," Aya says, flicking her fingers over the waterfall menu. The golden ramp retracts. Teagan's heart flutters a little when she sees Aya select the word 'Love.' A pink, petal-strewn path appears.

Teagan blushes. "You have time to show me around? I honestly didn't think I'd get a chance to talk with you tonight. You're the star of the show. I would have thought you'd be tied up with VIPs."

Aya threads her arm through Teagan's and whispers to her conspiratorially, "You are a VIP. You are an old friend and an important investor."

Teagan feels more like a schoolchild than a VIP. *My legs are trembling.*

They step onto the path and the wall of water closes behind them. Teagan concentrates hard on not tripping or spilling her drink. The volume of the music increases to the point where it is pounding inside her. The overstimulation—and proximity to Aya—makes her feel drunk.

Teagan wants to kiss Aya. She imagines embracing her, being kissed back. *Don't be an idiot*, Teagan chides herself. *She's not into you. She's just being kind.*

A rounded archway looms. Aya leads Teagan through it into a cave-like room. Eight blissed-out-looking people in headdresses sit around a glowing hub. The whole room pulses with a pink light. The headdresses the people wear remind Teagan of Grecian laurel leaves. "What am I looking at Aya?"

Aya smiles proudly. "This is Aphrodite. This program counteracts negative feedback we absorb from our parents, teachers, lovers, and other well-meaning but harmful influences."

"It teaches you how to love yourself?"

"It does not teach," Aya corrects. "It overwrites our behavioral programming, replacing the negative feedback loop we have internalized with a positive one. After fifteen minutes, each of these people will have an increased capacity for self-understanding and acceptance that will allow them to be more compassionate to themselves."

"I wish I'd had one of those when I was fifteen," Teagan jokes. "How long does the positive feeling last?" *What Aya is doing with Kakumei is noble. Neural Nirvana helps people.* Teagan feels a stab of jealousy. NeuroNet began as something pure, too. But since hearing about Dee, it all feels tainted somehow.

Aya takes her time before responding. "That depends on the length of time spent with the device and the number of sessions. Results are cumulative. If they only experience Neural Nirvana tonight, they will feel good for a couple of days. But after time spent with a negative person of importance, they will need another session."

"Like a micromanaging boss?" Teagan laughs. "Or a jealous spouse?"

Aya flashes a wry smile. "Everyone who hurts us means well, do they not?"

"Not everyone." Teagan wants to tell Aya about everything: her doubts about uploading Em, her fears about Dee. *Aya would understand in a way the boys can't.* But they're not alone. And she doesn't want to dump her personal problems on Aya. *It's a big night that she should enjoy.* She deposits her empty glass with a butler Eye.

Aya squeezes her arm. "Come, I want to show you Amy." She steers Teagan to a green room where several men float in immersion tanks with masks and bodysuits. "This is a full-body treatment," Aya explains. "In addition to calming brain waves, Amy aims to transform fast-twitch reactions to slow ones, completely rewiring the trigger, thought, action, and judgment behavior cycle."

"Is Amy short for amygdala?" Teagan isn't as up on her neurobiology as Aya, but she does remember that's where the human 'fight or flight' impulse originates.

Aya nods.

This is a weird scene. The men floating in the tanks with glowing headdresses look like they are waiting for someone to harvest their organs. "Amy is capable of manipulating their involuntary stress reactions?"

"To overwrite old conditioning that triggered stress, anxiety, and the entire range of fight or flight reactions, as well as emotional excesses, like rage. The fluid is sedative; the headdress is conductive."

"Amy is able to suppress rage impulses?"

Aya smiles. "No, no. Neural Nirvana suppresses nothing. It is important for people to access all feelings. On their own feelings are neither good nor bad. They simply are. For example, conflict drives change and innovation. You do not want to suffocate that. All I am doing is working to transform potentially destructive impulses into productive ones. Overwriting the core programming. Correcting nature's defects with a human-centered approach to technology."

Teagan gestures to the floating men. "Where'd you get so many test subjects?"

"The state is incredibly supportive of my research. We are betting Amy will be able to end mass incarcerations. Maybe one day she will replace the need to have a prison system at all."

She couldn't be using . . . "These human trials? Are you using criminals as test subjects?"

"They will not be criminals for long," Aya says.

Teagan wonders if they'd volunteered or been voluntold to participate.

"Amy is helping them gain impulse control. Soon the Neural Network therapy will completely overwrite the ingrained patterns of behavior that caused them to make bad choices and we will be able to reintroduce them into society."

"Are they hardened criminals?" Teagan eyes the submerged men warily, hoping no rapists or murderers wake up.

"Do not worry." Aya points to a mirrored wall. "They are being monitored by security."

Teagan feels a little better. "I know you're early-stage, but what you're building here is impressive." That gives her an idea. "Aya, do you think your tech would work on Model Twos?"

Aya's countenance freezes. "If Carter had let me ungate the AI, they would. But your uploads are frozen in time. My tech is about becoming your best self. I doubt your machines have the capacity for growth. You can thank Carter for that. What a waste."

Time hasn't dulled Aya's resentment. *She sounds just as bitter as Carter,* Teagan notes. "What if we ungate the AI?"

"It is possible." Aya says. "But I do not want to talk about ancient history. I want to show you something new. It is a prosumer version of Amy to liberate people from the crippling effects of depression and anxiety. I am planning to release a mobile version for Christmas that uses a lower dose of Amy-type therapy to help people lose weight, sleep better, be more social, give up alcohol . . . all those New Year Resolution-type things that require behavioral modification. I call it Janus."

Teagan wants to stay, but a quick glance at a nearby Eye confirms it's time to go. "All of that sounds amazing, and I'd love to see it, but I can't tonight. I promised Em I'd be home by ten. I need to get going."

"You must have had a very long day," Aya says, voice lowering. "I saw the news about Dee Claybourne. So scary. I hope it is just a glitch. Do you want to take one of my headdresses home? It might help you relax."

"Relaxation isn't what I need." Teagan scans the room. "How do I get back to the valet from here?"

"Take it for Em, then?" Aya seems oblivious to Teagan's attempts to leave. "Is she responding well to treatment?"

Teagan snaps. "She's dying." As Aya's eyes widen, Teagan back-pedals. "I'm sorry. That didn't come out right."

Aya waves it off. "You are under a lot of stress. Em must be, too. I can send something with you that will help her come to peace with the situation and let go."

Teagan says, "If anyone needs to let go, it's me."

"If you stop holding on to everything you carry so tightly, you might actually discover who you really are." Aya's laugh reminds Teagan of birdsong. "I miss working with you." Aya embraces Teagan. She smells like cherry blossoms, and where Teagan's body touches hers, it tingles. Aya releases her, holding Teagan at arm's length. "Maybe you should let go and live a little. I would be interested in seeing who you become."

Teagan isn't sure how to respond, so she says nothing. An Eye leads her out of the party to the valet. The emotions of the day catch up with her on the ride home. *I'm wiped out.* She flicks on autopilot and takes a nap. As the car winds its way home, Teagan dreams of Aya's quick embrace. But in her dream, the embrace happens repeatedly. She plays out different scenarios. *This is what would have happened if I'd kissed Aya's cheek, or lingered longer, or ran my tongue across her lips . . .*

Teagan wakes as the car descends. She stumbles through her garage, half-awake. She's completely wiped out. She presses her palm against the biometric lock and nearly falls asleep in the seconds it takes to scan her prints and unlock the door.

All the lights are on. "Em?" *What a waste of money.* Squinting puts Teagan in a foul mood. *Why can't Em remember to turn the lights off? It's not that hard.* Teagan wonders if she can add a program patch to Em's upload that will force her to turn lights off when she exits rooms. "Em, I'm home!"

No answer.

Teagan finds Em curled up, asleep on the couch. Despite the illness, Em still looks beautiful sleeping. Teagan presses her lips to Em's forehead. *Her flesh is on fire.* Teagan draws back, concerned. Em's pulse beats an irregular pattern. Her breath is coming fast and shallow. *Something's wrong.* Teagan is wide awake now.

7

Teagan hates this hospital. Its rooms are too small. Its staff smiles while delivering shocking news. Teagan tries not to sigh too heavily as the nurse checks all the bags and monitors attached to her wife. "How long until we can go?"

"An hour? Maybe two?" the nurse says.

"Really?" Not that Teagan will argue, she is happy to go. But that seems awfully quick. "Em was in bad shape a few hours ago."

"We need to get two more liters of fluid in her system and then she should be fine." The nurse smiles. "It's good you brought her in when you did. Treatments often suppress the immune system. When you or I get an infection, it's no big deal. But when an immunocompromised body like hers gets dehydrated, everything starts to shut down. The smallest infection can become fatal."

"A glass of water could have prevented this?" Teagan's brow creases. That sounds so stupid.

"Yes." The nurse detaches an empty fluid bag and hooks up its replacement. "Make sure she drinks at least sixty-four ounces of water a day. If she argues, ask her if she wants to come back and see me. I guarantee she won't."

Teagan mentally thanks whatever god is on duty tonight that they only have to get Em to drink water to avoid this happening again. The devil in her thinks, *Although it would have saved us both a lot of trouble if she died of natural causes.*

The nurse waves and promises to return in an hour or so. Teagan is thankful no one can hear her thoughts. She tries to get comfortable on the narrow bench by the bed. It's so cramped, her knees rub against the bed's curved safety rails. *But I don't deserve to be comfortable. I was flirting while she was suffering.* She clasps Em's fingers through the rails and squeezes three times. Em coughs, but her eyes remain closed. Teagan extracts a tissue from her purse and wipes a clot of blood from Em's lips.

There is a knock at the door. Carter peaks around its edge. "Can I come in?" Teagan nods, glad to see him.

Carter pauses at the foot of Em's bed. "Jesus. She doesn't even look like herself anymore."

"I know. I try not to look too closely. It's easier to think of how she was before."

Carter squeezes her shoulder. "Her shell will have better color. Tito can use an old photo to match the skin tone to when Em was healthy."

Teagan shrugs. She's not concerned about that. "Can you believe this emergency was caused by dehydration? Of all the things that could have gone wrong, she didn't drink enough water."

"What?" His face crinkles in confusion. "That's nuts. Why won't she drink water?"

"She doesn't like the taste."

Carter laughs at the absurdity.

His laughter catches Teagan off-guard. *It is funny.* She begins to laugh, too, until tears run down her face. When she catches her breath, she says, "I feel horrible laughing."

"Don't. It's absurd." Carter wipes tears from his own eyes. "Hey, scoot over." He squeezes into the space beside her and takes her hand. "What are you going to do now?"

Carter's hand in hers is an anchor. For the first time all day, Teagan feels grounded. "We can leave soon. Then I think we should upload Em as soon as possible."

Carter's brows knit. "We haven't finished her body. Where do you want to store the consciousness?"

Teagan shrugs. "We can house her in an Eye like we used to with the Model Ones. It'll be a good short-term fix until we have a shell ready."

"No second thoughts? Not having a skin is a good excuse if you—"

"If I want to let her die? No, I must upload her," Teagan says. She smirks. "If I don't, I'd have to start dating again. And then I'd have to break in someone new. It's too much trouble."

Dating does feel terrifying. *I've been with Em since high school. I've never slept with anyone else. Who else would want me?* Afraid she sounded callous, she adds, "All jokes aside, it's the right thing to do."

Carter doesn't argue. He nods and says, "That might be for the best."

That's not like him. Teagan waits, but he adds nothing. *Something's up.* "What?"

Carter shifts uncomfortably. "You weren't answering your phone . . . So, I stopped by your house, but you were already here, so I came over . . . I wanted to tell you in person . . ."

Teagan swallows. Her throat is dry. "Tell me what?"

Carter scratches the side of his ring finger. Teagan recognizes the tic. *He has sad news.* She wants a cup of water. But she can't move until she hears what's wrong. "Tell me what?"

He sighs. "I shouldn't have gone home, but I told Rhys I'd be back for dinner, and you know how she is . . ."

"I know. She loves her Daddy." Rhys is Teagan's goddaughter, Carter's child. She'd be turning twenty soon if she hadn't been uploaded. As it is, she's finishing her twelfth year of being eight years old. Teagan can't think of that without remembering the awful day they lost Rhys's mother. Melody was dead on arrival. Not that it stopped Carter from trying to upload her. Teagan studies Carter's face in the harsh hospital room light. Deep worry lines crease his face. *I wonder if he'd be any happier if he had two loved ones to come home to instead of one?*

Carter looks down. "Tito was scanning the dashboards and saw a bot blink out. He did some digging, and we were able to retrieve the footage."

The knot in Teagan's chest is back. "Footage of what?"

Carter's eyes meet hers. "A bot suicide, Teagan. At least it looks that way."

All the hairs along Teagan's arms stand on end. "What do you mean 'a bot suicide'?" She glances at Em, but of course her wife isn't listening. She's barely conscious. "What happened?"

"Tito recovered the footage from the Ravenswood El train in Chicago. There's a portion of the track you can walk over, a short way from the platform. The loved one just stood on the tracks, waiting for the train to come and hit it."

"Jesus." Teagan shivers. *What's the old saying? Someone is walking over my grave.* "We need to postpone all uploads, Em included."

Carter shakes his head. "I don't think we should do that."

"Carter!" Teagan drops his hand. "I don't know if this is an isolated incident or some kind of Dee Claybourne copycat, but if there is a chance of other bots following suit, we need to pause the procedures until we know what's going on."

"I have a better idea."

Teagan frowns. She can count the times his ideas were better than hers on both hands. "Enlighten me."

"If we pause, we need to alert the investors. Even if everyone is under an NDA, someone will leak to the media. I don't want people to panic."

She knows why he's concerned. He's behind the fundraising goal already. If anyone else pulls out, they might as well cancel the IPO. "What do you suggest?"

"We keep uploading people, but we single out particular cases of interest." Carter's eyes drift toward Em's wasted frame.

Teagan's stomach flips unpleasantly. "What do you mean?"

"We should identify any factor that might trigger an eventual suicide," he says. "For example, mental disorders."

"Em's bipolar." Teagan feels her shoulders tighten. "That doesn't mean she's suicidal."

"Of course not!" Carter takes her hands again. "But it's a risk factor. So, we upload Em and put her under tighter surveillance than normal. But we also watch other risk factors, like uploads in families with significant debt or drug-abuse issues."

"You'd be able to get my consent," Teagan says. "But it might take two weeks for legal to review the release forms."

Carter's mouth twists. "We don't need release forms."

"To do the kind of monitoring you're talking about? We certainly do."

"It's our data," Carter says.

He's right. But it still feels rotten. "And we don't inform the guardians? Even though we'd be monitoring them, too?"

Carter purses his lips. He always does this when he wants her to stop questioning him. "We're already monitoring them around the clock. But we don't look closely at the data unless something goes wrong. The only thing we'd be doing differently is paying attention to the data and analyzing it in real time for a select group of individuals. What don't you like?"

Teagan sighs. "I don't like keeping secrets."

"They're already providing all the data we need."

"That's not what I'm talking about." She searches for the words to articulate what she finds unsettling. "I don't like knowing that we're looking for time bombs. We're identifying potential threats. That's good. But instead of neutralizing them, we're waiting for them to explode. We need to warn the guardians of any potential danger."

"No." Carter's eyes plead with her. "Until we know what we're looking for, what the true threats are, what would we tell them? It would only freak them out and skew the results."

"But you want to experiment on Em and you just told me." Teagan fights the tears that are welling up. "That's not going to freak me out and skew the results?"

"You're not going to lose Em twice." Carter pulls Teagan to him and wraps his arms around her heaving shoulders. "I promise."

8

Em leans against the kitchen counter and peers at Teagan over her sixty-four-ounce water bottle. "Why do you keep pacing?"

Teagan stops. "Sorry. I didn't realize I was. I was thinking about the boys. Wondering how they're getting on without me." It's not what she's really thinking, but she can't tell Em: *You're about to become a science experiment. One that might self-destruct in ways we can't predict for reasons we can't explain.* Em looks much better, but Teagan asks, "How are you feeling?"

Em's brow creases. "The same as I did five minutes ago." She grimaces at the giant water bottle. "Honestly, do I have to finish this whole thing?"

This is a question Em's been asking every five minutes. Teagan crosses her arms. "You don't want to end up back in the hospital, do you?"

Em groans. "What does it matter if I'm hydrated or not? I'm just going to be uploaded anyway. I can barely lift this thing to my lips."

"Then it will help you build muscle mass."

Em rolls her eyes. "Because that will be so useful when I'm in a synthetic body." She takes a sip of water. "Ugh. Gross."

Teagan shakes her head. "I can't believe you hate the taste of water. It's water. It has no taste."

"That's what makes it so disgusting."

Teagan scratches the back of her neck, where she can feel muscles starting to knot. "Do you want a flavor tablet? I picked some up in the gift shop."

"What flavors do you have?"

"Hibiscus?"

Em's pretty lips curl. "Tastes like soap."

Why does Em make everything so difficult? "Strawberry?"

"Too sweet."

One last option. If she doesn't like this, I'll just pour the whole jug down her throat. "Lime?" Teagan tenses.

Em smiles. "I'll take lime."

Teagan's shoulders relax. "It's a good thing I got three options."

"You know me too well." Em pulls her closer and says, "I'm sorry I'm such a pain in the ass."

Teagan's anger dissolves as quickly as the water tablet. *I don't want to waste one of her loving moods.* "You're not a pain in the ass. You're a very discerning individual in a demanding situation. There's a difference."

Em kisses Teagan's cheek. "Thank you."

"For what?" Teagan, exhausted, sits.

Em drops the jug on the table. "For making me drink gallons and gallons of water." She lifts the hem of her robe and sits astride Teagan's lap, throwing her arms around Teagan's neck. "Seriously, though, thank you for taking such loving care of me. I know it's not easy."

When Em is this close, Teagan has trouble thinking. She smiles at Em's beautiful lips. "You're the one doing all the work."

"Bullshit," Em says, tugging one of Teagan's curls.

It hurts, but Teagan holds her tongue. She wants a kiss and does not want to drive it away. A thousand days of wanting claw their way up her spine. Her lips find the hollow of Em's neck.

Em sighs. Teagan kisses her with more urgency, afraid the mood will pass before she can find release. Em looks down at her and laughs. "When you kiss me after I'm uploaded, will I still feel it?"

Teagan rises, lifting Em with her and gestures for the Eye to sweep the table clean. This is a tale best punctuated with kisses. "It will be different." She gently places Em down and undoes the haphazardly tied robe. There is a freckle above Em's navel. Teagan bends to kiss it. "But I've been told it's pleasurable."

Em arches. Encouraged, Teagan traces pathways she thought had been closed to her, beginning with the divot of Em's hip. "You'll have a nerve layer underneath the bot skin." The soft curve of Em's flank requires loving attention. "It will send electrical impulses that your central processor will translate into actions, impulses, sensations."

Em pulls Teagan's head up by the hair. Teagan wants to scream, but she holds it in. She doesn't want to lose access to Em's heavenly body. Em props herself up on an elbow and asks, "Will you still want to kiss me when I'm a bot?"

Teagan knows the skin will feel like skin, the temperature of the body and the viscosity of the liquids will be the same as what she knows, but part of her recoils at the thought of having sex with an android. She doesn't say that, though. Instead, she says, "I will kiss you whenever, wherever you want."

Em's eyes fill with tears. "I'm scared."

Teagan is overwhelmed. Em never admits fear. Never succumbs to defeat. "Don't be." Teagan scrambles on top of the table and gathers her into her arms. "I'm here. I'll always be here for you." Teagan takes Em's face into her hands and finally gets the kiss she's been craving.

A mood, deep and heaving, rolls over them. It sweeps them up and mashes them together. They are one body and spirit. Every drop of love they can muster oozes out onto the cool marble top of the kitchen table. When Teagan finally comes up for air, she clasps Em tightly to her chest. They lay there, damp and heaving, riding waves of feeling.

It used to be like this all the time, Teagan thinks. She wonders if all love affairs follow this trajectory: a brief, fiery beginning followed by endlessly vague years of middling quality? And then what? A tragic, volcanic end? Or something even more boring? *Maybe I'm the boring one. Maybe her life would be better if I hadn't forced her to stay with me.*

Teagan studies Em's profile in the golden light of a fading day. "I don't blame you for being scared," she whispers. "I'd be scared, too, if being uploaded meant putting up with me until I died."

Em pinches Teagan's arm, wrinkles her nose, and whispers back, "I don't put up with you. I love you."

Teagan's eyes fill with tears. Not because she believes Em. But because for once, it almost sounds like Em means it.

Teagan carries Em upstairs. She watches Em fall asleep, then dream. In the morning, she smiles, listening to her wife's gentle snores. *Last night was nice. We can have more nights like this. If I engineer a better solution.* She considers the options. *Could we program out Em's mood swings? Maybe ungate her AI and partner with Neural Nirvana to overwrite Em's ingrained behaviors?*

Teagan chews her lip. *Would that skew the experiment?*

Maybe we need to create alpha, beta, and control versions of Em? NeuroNet has enough storage space to hold a triplicate upload.

But where would we house them? Only one body has been ordered. And even that one won't be ready when we complete the upload. Em's consciousness will have to live in the household's Eye until the body comes in.

And if we have a beta and a control, they need to all go into operation at the same time. Otherwise, how would Tito track its evolution or decay patterns?

Em moans. Teagan chuckles. *On second thought, I can barely handle one Em . . . what would I do with three?*

She thinks of the painful pleasure that's still imprinted on her body from the long night before. *Do I really want a kind and docile Em? Em is maddening, unpredictable, and untrustworthy. What would be left of her if I cut those qualities out? Would I be able to love what is left?*

Teagan touches the curve of Em's jaw. Em bats her hand away. Teagan lifts the blanket and pulls Em on top of her chest. Teagan lets her hands dance gently along Em's spine. Her fingers move slowly. Teagan wants to memorize this moment. She wants to remember Em like this: worn out from pleasure, soft, beautiful, and frail. She wants to linger in this moment: arms wrapped around each other like a couple in love. Teagan realizes this is a memory that might have to last her forever. That stings worse than the tears.

9

Monday morning is full of ugly, wet clouds. But Em is practically glowing. "Upload day," she cheerfully announces. "The first day of my new life."

Teagan smiles, but she doesn't share Em's high spirits. "At least it's not a Tuesday." *I need all the luck I can get.* "You're not nervous?"

"No," Em stretches and groans. "I won't miss this body, but I wish I had one to go into."

"The Eye's just a temporary home," Teagan says. "Then we can transfer you into your shell." She gestures to the household Eye that will travel with them to the lab. "At least it's rose gold . . . Your favorite color."

Em laughs. "I was just about to say that!"

Teagan presses her lips to Em's. "I'm going to miss this mouth."

Em's amber eyes smile, full of mischief. "Will you, really?"

Teagan laughs. "The mouth, yes. The arguments issuing from it, no."

Hours later, it's surreal to see Em on a slab, hooked to Tito's efficient web of tubes and wires. He tells her, "You can wait in the guardian's lobby."

Teagan shakes her head. "That feels wrong. I need to be here."

Tito nods and completes the set-up.

In twilight sleep, Em already looks dead, her face waxy, sallow, and sunken. The rose-gold Eye strapped into the surgical cot beside looks comical. "It's hard to believe a whole human being can fit inside something so small."

Tito laughs. "Imagine if we used more than ten percent of our brain." He adjusts the settings on his console. "Ready?"

Teagan nods, then stops him. "Can I say goodbye?"

"Of course."

Teagan takes Em's hand, trying not to think of how cold and dry it feels and squeezes it three times. She doesn't expect anything in return, but the lack of response sinks a stone in her belly. She knows Em hears nothing, but she tells her, "I love you." Because it's better than not saying anything at all. And ritual demands something. A hand squeezes her shoulder. It's Carter. "You came?"

"Of course."

Teagan hugs him.

"Here we go," Tito says. He pushes his glasses above his magic eyebrows. "Uploading commencing."

Carter slings an arm around Teagan's shoulders and squeezes her tight. "She's going to be fine."

Teagan sighs. "I know. It's just . . ." The dark circles under his eyes look darker. "I wish we could have saved Melody. It doesn't seem fair that Em gets a chance we couldn't give her."

"That's not fair." Carter's eyes pinken. He swipes at them with his free arm. "I'm supposed to be comforting you."

Teagan reddens. "Sorry. I didn't mean—"

"I know," Carter says, cutting her off. "I was thinking about her, too."

Tito glances at the monitor. "We're at sixty percent. Projected time to one hundred percent is nine minutes and fifty-five seconds."

Teagan whistles low. "You've really accelerated your pace of play." The upload process used to take the better part of a day.

Tito chuckles and scans the dashboard. "Systems normal. No anomalies. No charted dissonance."

Teagan can't help herself. "Em not causing dissonance is unusual." The boys giggle. Teagan watches the countdown on Tito's dashboard.

"Seriously, it's been a minute since I've observed the procedure. I can't believe it goes so fast."

Tito shrugs. "I've had twelve years to tweak Aya's mind-mapping process. Imbuing it with AI is what really speeded things up."

"Still, it would take me longer to get a cavity filled than upload Em's forty-five years of experiences. What you've done is incredible."

Tito's chest puffs out a bit, straining against his lab coat, although he says modestly, "It's a team effort."

Carter smirks. "And we didn't want to give you time to change your mind."

Teagan laughs a little louder and harder than she means to as his joke lands. "It's true," she admits. "That's probably a good thing." She watches the lights twinkling across the skullcap of wires affixed to Em's temples. Each one is an electrical impulse representing a choice, memory, action, habit, connection, or thought.

Is that all we are, data points?

If so, Em is nearly empty.

Guardians often ask what gets left out when their loved one is uploaded. The standard answer is nothing. But Teagan knows feelings can't be mapped, even though the actions and reactions they cause can. Recreating the semblance of feeling is something she spent most of her research and development time on. Sensors in the outer membrane of the loved one's 'skin' transmit messages to the central core processor. From there, a memory is matched, a reaction provoked. But it's different from feeling. And when the upload is in the Eye, the loved one doesn't even have that.

"Data transfer is at one hundred percent," Tito says. "I'm going to start the rendering and backup check. Time to completion: fifteen minutes. Then we can euthanize."

Fifteen minutes. Em has fifteen minutes of life left. Teagan thinks Em already looks dead. In the neighboring surgical bed, the rose-gold Eye hums as Tito double-checks the uploaded data.

She doesn't mean to, but the strapped-down Eye reminds her again of Rhys and Melody. All the Model One uploads were stored in Eyes. *Rhys was only seven.* Teagan can't picture what a nineteen-year-old Rhys would look like. Then she realizes, *She'd probably look like Melody.*

Teagan steals a glance at Carter and wonders if that's one of the reasons why he fought so hard against letting loved ones evolve. After the Model Twos came online, Carter based Rhys's synthetic shell on old family photographs. He manipulated the designs himself until she was perfect. *A perfect child who'll never grow up.*

Rhys was the first child NeuroNet uploaded. Aya wanted to use her as a test case. "Let me ungate her AI," she had begged, "let her evolve."

"Evolve into what?" Carter shot back. "I don't want to lose my daughter again."

Aya argued the ethics of forcing a child to stay a child forever. Carter's point of view was that the child was dead, so the concern should be placed on the guardian's state of mind. "If you give the AI free rein, we have no control over who Rhys will become. Keep her gated and I'll always have my baby. I want to recognize who she is as she gets older."

Aya pointed out that doing that would prevent Rhys from getting older, but Carter didn't care. Tito sided with Carter. If the loved one aged, then their body should too. "We don't have the resources required to upgrade the hardware more than once or twice."

Teagan agreed that would be a headache. "People have enough trouble recycling batteries. What are we supposed to do with discarded android shells? And how can we age them? We can have AI predict how a person might age, but we don't know with any certainty if we'd be right or not."

Teagan had always backed Aya up. Aya's science was perfect. And privately, Teagan agreed with Aya—ungating the AI for Rhys was the most humane solution. But Carter was her best friend. And Tito was right: changing out the shells every few years would create a logistical nightmare.

Aya didn't understand and she wouldn't compromise or yield. She resigned that afternoon.

If Teagan had known that decision would drive Aya out of NeuroNet completely, she would have fought harder to keep her. She might have even argued with Carter that ungating the AI and letting Rhys evolve was the way to go. But Teagan hadn't. She'd backed the boys. Aya was gone before Rhys's upload finished processing.

Teagan rubs her eyes with a hand and tries to refocus on the now. But Em's unresponsive body with its colorful cap reminds her again of Melody. Teagan shudders, remembering the limp body Carter should have sent to the morgue. She'd been killed on impact. No one should have let him drag Melody into the lab. Even if she was his wife, someone should have stopped him.

Instead, the small contingent of first responders had followed Carter into the building. As he hooked Melody's corpse up to the NeuroNet, they stood there, looking at their boots, shuffling around the perimeter of the lab. Everyone knew there was no pulse. But Carter was Neuro-Net's co-founder. They must have assumed that he knew what he was doing. Teagan knew he must have been mad with grief. Otherwise, he'd never have tried to upload after brain death.

Em is the one laying on the slab, but Teagan remembers how Melody laid there, vacant eyes staring up at the ceiling, blood congealing around gashes on her face and neck from flying through the windshield.

Teagan had recognized signs of rigor mortis beginning to tighten Melody's hands into hooks. But when she tried to stop Carter, he cut her off and ordered her to process Rhys. Teagan and Tito had loaded Rhys's tiny body onto the second slab in the bay. But the whole situation felt wrong. Melody had been quick with a joke, full of life. Nothing of that human being remained. "Tito," she had whispered. "We can't let him try."

Tito had shrugged. "But what if it works? That opens a whole new window of customers."

Am I being silly? Teagan had wondered. Tito and Carter had proceeded as if Melody was a typical upload, not a scientific experiment on a corpse.

Tito had activated both caps to begin the upload procedure. The one on Rhys began to flicker with a rainbow array of colors. Predictably, no activity registered on Melody's.

Carter had gestured to Tito to cut the current to Melody's cap so he could adjust it. "Again," he said. Tito obliged. Still nothing.

Teagan had tried to intercede again. Carter shushed her and shooed Tito away from the board. He cut the current, slathered more gel on the sensors, reapplied the cap, and switched the power back on.

Carter ignored Teagan's attempt to get his attention. He fetched a new cap, disconnected the old one and replaced it before repeating the same exercise.

That time, Teagan had tried to physically restrain him. "Carter," she said. "Melody is dead. There's no neural activity to upload."

Instead of responding to her, Carter had simply walked out of the lab. Tito and Teagan disconnected the NeuroNet apparatus and let the paramedics take Melody's body away.

What might have changed if he had been successful? Teagan wonders.

Tito's voice snaps Teagan back to the present. "Processing complete." He removes the neural cap and respirator from Em's body. "Do you want to say anything before we euthanize?"

Teagan nods, surprised at the lump forming in her throat. "I feel stupid I didn't prepare anything."

"Well, it's not like she can hear you," Carter quips. Tito shoots him an annoyed look. He holds out his hands, "What? Too soon?"

Teagan laughs despite herself. "Yes!" She takes Em's face in her hands. "Goodnight, Em." Em's lips are cold, but still soft. "I'll see you on the other side."

She tries to memorize the planes of Em's face. Teagan knows that the manufactured shell will look healthier than this cancer-eaten body, but she wants to remember this human element, as broken as it is.

Tito fastens a different breathing apparatus over Em's mouth and nose. Carter twists a nob on a cannister. Pure nitrogen is a humane way to euthanize this empty body. Within two breaths, Em will be out. From there, suffocation will be quick and relatively painless.

Teagan, Tito and Carter researched countless ways to euthanize before settling on nitrogen. It is the most elegant solution.

10

Carter teasingly holds out a copy of the *NeuroNet Guardian's Manual*. "I recommend you read this during the first twenty-four hours of care."

Teagan smacks him before taking it. "As if I didn't write the damn thing."

A smile tugs at the corner of his mouth. "Then you should adjust well to your new role."

Teagan feels Tito's hand squeeze her shoulder. "Seriously though, how are you?"

"Weird." Teagan wants to laugh, but her thoughts are all over the place. "I'm used to giving these orientations, not sitting through them. And you're failing to bolster me. I don't feel confident or comfortable at all."

"Well, if you're not ready to become a Guardian, we can always wipe the Eye's new content and restore it to factory settings." Carter looks downright impish.

"Don't you dare!"

Tito scowls. "Seriously, mate. Bad taste!"

Carter winks. "You've got to admit it would be a great practical joke."

"Would it really?" Tito doesn't sound convinced. He looks annoyed.

Teagan feels too empty to be upset. It's sweet that Tito's upset for her. "Carter, you've been a guardian for a long time, is there anything that isn't in the manual that I should know?"

He shrugs. "Nothing that you won't be able to figure out."

Tito's brow furrows, wobbling the glasses shoved above it. "Actually," he says, "as a test case, there's additional information you should know—"

"Or not," Carter interrupts. "I'd prefer she proceed like a typical guardian."

Teagan registers Tito's concern and Carter's belligerence. "I don't like being kept in the dark."

Carter's chin juts out. "And I don't like skewing test results."

Teagan is over this. "Fine. Is Em ready to take home?"

Carter looks disappointed. "You don't want to come over for dinner? It's Friday."

Friday is their long-standing 'date' night. Teagan shakes her head. "I don't think that's a good idea."

"Why not?" Carter's eyes glint with mischief. "It's not like Em can get mad. Or feel jealous you're spending time with me."

Despite herself, Teagan laughs. "Em not able to rage anymore? That's a dream come true." The dark part of her mind adds, *Too bad all she had to do was die first.* She shakes that thought off. "But I'm not feeling myself. I don't know if I'd be particularly good company. Besides, I should probably get Em settled at home."

Tito steadies his glasses. "Not much settling to do. She's already integrated into the Eye's firmware. Just turn her on at home."

Carter leans forward. "And if you don't turn her on until you get home from dinner, how will she ever know how long you took before you booted her up?"

Teagan frowns, considering the ethics. *If Em has no feelings to hurt, then does it make sense to say no? After all, I'm the one who's still alive.*

"You've been through so much," Carter says. "Let me take care of you. You deserve a little fun. And Rhys misses you."

Teagan can't help smirking at that. *Rhys can't miss me any more than Em can get angry.* But she does enjoy their company. *And this has been a hell of a week.* "Okay, you loser. I'll come after I finish the paperwork for the morgue and collect the Eye."

Thankfully, one of Tito's technicians removed Em's body. All that's left in the bay is the Eye: dormant, shiny, and rose-tinted.

Teagan touches the Eye's cool exterior. "This will be your new home for the next couple of months." She lifts the Eye. It's barely heavier than an overnight bag. *It's amazing that this is all a life weighs.* She clutches it to her chest as she walks down the hall, avoiding eye contact with any of the NeuroNet staff. She doesn't want to have to explain. She doubts any of these employees remember when uploads went home in Eyes. And those that do would wonder why it's not activated and trailing behind her. *I'm glad I'm waiting to bring her back. I need time to process and grieve.*

The elevator doors close, and Teagan realizes she must have been holding her breath. She slips her thumb in the security pad and the elevator skips all the floors between the lab and the Executive Suite. As it hurtles upward, she depresses the car fob in her pocket, calling her car to the roof. Carter's probably already on his way home, but she hurries outside in case he's still at his workstation. If he made a joke now, she doesn't think she could bear it.

The door to the car slides away and she settles Em-in-the-Eye into the passenger seat. Tenderly, she fastens the seatbelt around it before her own. She has time to drop Em off at home, but that doesn't feel right. Instead, she keys in a few destinations. "I want to visit our greatest hits," she tells the Eye. She and Em will visit all the sites that once held meaning for them. "It's not much," Teagan admits, "but I'll do it again when you have a body so you can enjoy it." First, Teagan wants to try and remember how she and Em began. Why they fell in love. And what it meant. Before life got in the way.

11

Carter Smith's house looms over a traditional cul-de-sac. Even in a neighborhood full of McMansions, his home stands out. Its massive ivory pillars warn neighbors not to come too close.

Melody always hated it. "Our friends are going to think we've become jerks," she'd said when Carter purchased it from an old money heir. But she endured it because of Carter and had tried to make it a warm and welcoming place.

Teagan knows why he went so big. It was what all the other Tech Village entrepreneurs did once they came into a little money: buy a big house outside the Perimeter and a flying car to reduce the commute. She can see the Alabama border from his second-floor window, but it doesn't matter. With his car, he can be downtown in thirty minutes.

Teagan scans the horizon. The only thing she likes about Northwest Georgia is the mountain ridge that rolls from here across the Tennessee border. In the light of the full moon, the mountains shimmer dark purple and green against a bruised sky. These mountains were here before the tech bros, and they'll outlive them. Just as they buried the farmers who once worked on this land. Before the farmers, they sheltered Indigenous peoples who hunted in their shadows. Under their benevolent watch, life first clambered out of the rivers and learned to walk. And before that, these peaks exploded into being from the ocean floor itself. She likes contemplating things that men can't touch.

The car begins its descent. Teagan wishes she had the mountains' calm. *Maybe without the tempests and storms of my relationship with Em,*

I can be more Zen? The Em-in-the-Eye jiggles against its seat restraint. Teagan is tempted to never activate it.

The car bumps softly to the ground. Teagan pats Em's spherical shell and whispers, "We're here." She delicately undoes the restraints and carries Em-in-the-Eye to the grand entrance. Teagan's biometric information could open the front door, but she rings the bell. Rhys loves greeting her. And Teagan enjoys their ritual.

"Aunt Teagan!" Rhys cries. Her chubby arms lift but she stops short of embracing her godmother. "Why do you have an Eye? Why isn't it on?"

Teagan blushes and darts a glance at Carter, who's entered the foyer. She hadn't thought of how to explain Em's loss to Rhys. She considers what might make sense to a seven-year-old. "It's your Auntie Em. I didn't want to leave her home."

Carter's eyebrow lifts. "You couldn't leave her in the car?"

Teagan shrugs. "I guess I could, but it felt rude, somehow."

"Okay you weirdo," Carter says with a laugh. "Em's always been invited to dinner before. Might as well bring her in. You hungry?"

Teagan's stomach growls, reminding her she skipped lunch. "Yeah."

"Boot Em up, we'll have a family dinner." Carter laughs as he dodges Teagan's half-hearted attempt to slap him.

Rhys places her tiny hands on either side of the Eye and looks up with wide blue eyes. "What happened to Auntie Em?"

Teagan forces herself to smile. She brushes a curl back from Rhys's forehead. "She was in too much pain to live, so we had to put her to sleep."

Rhys strokes the Eye. "She's sleeping?"

"Yes." Teagan can't believe it's been twelve years since Rhys's upload. "You were in an Eye when we first did your transfer. Do you remember?"

Something inscrutable flickers across Rhys's face. Teagan wonders if she remembers the car crash, or if it was the constraints of the Eye causing that flash of discord. The child nods and says, "I didn't sleep, though."

"No, I guess you didn't." Teagan laughs. "Your Daddy couldn't wait to get you home and talk with you again." She tries to ignore the guilt cramping her gut. "But Em needs a little rest. When she wakes up again, all her pain will be gone. And she'll be a loved one, like you." She boops the child on the nose and kisses the top of her curly head.

Rhys smiles, giving Teagan the impression that the idea pleases her, and grips her hand. Teagan lets the small android child pull her across the foyer toward the dining room.

She stops to exchange a quick kiss with Carter. As her lips brush his cheek, they catch on stubble. The length of his beard is always a signal of his mental state. Tito keeps clean-shaven, no matter what's happening. But when Carter's hard-pressed, he pays little attention to hygiene. She didn't notice in the lab earlier, but he smells a little rank. Melody didn't have a sense of smell. Teagan used to tease Carter how lucky he was to have found a woman like that. She makes a mental note to remind him to shower before coming in to work tomorrow. Teagan notices the family dog is nowhere to be seen. That's unusual. Usually, they're all tripping over him. "Hey, where's Charlie?"

"Captain Underfoot hasn't been feeling so well this past week," Carter says.

"He's really tired," Rhys says. "He must need to go to sleep."

"Aw," Teagan says. "Poor guy. Is something wrong with him?"

"I think he's just old," Carter says. "He was our first kid."

"God, how old is he?"

"Almost twenty," Carter says.

Teagan's mouth drops open. "You're lucky he's still alive."

"I know he must not have much longer, but I don't know what I'll do when he dies." Carter loops his arm through Teagan's. "C'mon. Let's eat." He nods toward the Em-in-the-Eye Teagan holds in her hand. "Why don't you set her down?"

Teagan shakes her head. "Doesn't feel right."

Carter shrugs. "Suit yourself."

They walk down a short hallway to the dining room. The walls are lined with family photos, beginning with Carter and Teagan's high school days and ending with more current family portraits. Teagan smiles at the image of her and Em in fancy dresses. Her eye catches on a shot of her, Carter and Tito cutting the ribbon for the new offices. Aya was there, too, but Carter cut her out of the picture and put it in a smaller frame. After that come a series of family shots, beginning with Carter and Melody's engagement photo, then wedding shots, then formal annual pictures. At first, it's just the happy couple. Then baby Rhys makes an appearance. The chubby cherub grows each year until her seventh, and then there are only the two of them: Carter and Rhys. He keeps getting older, and she never changes. There are already twelve frames like that. Teagan wonders how many more years Carter will insist on capturing before he realizes how grotesque an exercise it is.

Rhys wants Teagan next to her. Teagan sets Em-in-the-Eye in the chair across and sits beside Rhys. Carter heads straight for the bar cart. "Scotch, neat?"

"Sure, but you could let the Eye do it," Teagan teases him.

"I don't like its portions." He gives each glass a generous pour. "Besides, why delay gratification?"

Teagan smirks at him. "They say doing so increases pleasure."

He hands her a cut crystal tumbler. "And who are these ubiquitous 'they?'"

"I'm not sure." She enjoys the way the scotch burns her throat. "But I am familiar with delayed gratification."

"In concept, of course. But has it made you happier?" Before Teagan can respond, the edges of Carter's mouth curl upward. "I'm not sure 'they' can be trusted. You know what else 'they' say."

Teagan laughs, happy to play. "Do I? I'm not sure I do. Can you enlighten me?"

"Stitch in time saves nine." Carter lifts an arm in a grand, dismissive gesture. "I mean, what are we to make of that? Or 'wool-gathering' . . . or 'early birds' and their worms . . ."

"By Jove, I think you're right." The scotch smooths Teagan's rough edges. "For example, they also say, 'Don't cry over spilt milk.' Rhys, what do you do when you spill milk?"

The child grins, looking happy to be part of the game. "I clean it up."

"That's right!" Teagan smacks the table for emphasis. "I've never cried, have you?"

Rhys giggles. "No!"

"Nor have I," Carter roars. He lifts his glass. Rhys takes up her tumbler of water. "To hell with 'them.'"

"To hell with them," Teagan and Rhys repeat.

The Eye descends, dishing out platters of roast chicken and vegetables. Teagan sips her scotch. Being here, at this table, with Carter and Rhys, feels like home. She sighs, content.

Carter clears his throat. "Penny for your thoughts?"

She smirks. "Isn't that what 'they' say?"

His grin is wide and wolfish. "Fuck them."

Rhys covers her ears. "Daddy!"

"Sorry, honey."

Teagan feels a twinge of sadness that Carter will never know Rhys as an adult woman. Her own relationship with her father deepened after college. *Carter will never know what that's like.* Being forced to teach and protect this eternal child, he'll never get the opportunity to learn who Rhys was meant to become.

Teagan stares at the Em-in-the-Eye sitting where her spouse should be. She downs the last of her drink and signals to Carter's Eye to bring another. Carter clears his throat and Teagan realizes he is waiting for a response. She smiles at him. "I was thinking of how much I enjoy my time with you both."

Rhys pats her arm with a chubby hand. "I love you, Aunt Teagan."

Teagan knows she sounds like she means it, but she doubts Rhys is capable of love anymore.

Carter smiles. "I love you, too, Teagan." She knows he does.

Teagan feels her heart jump to her throat. She swallows the tears and smiles a little too brightly. "Good. Now, let's eat."

12

It's much harder carrying Em-in-the-Eye after three scotches. Teagan stumbles into her own front door. Her momentum brings her too close to the biometric scanner. It warns her to back up. She does and nearly tips over backward from the weight of her wife's container. "I'm glad you can't see this," she whispers to the dormant Em-in-the-Eye.

After three tries and two aborted biometric scans, the door finally slides open. Teagan steps over the threshold. She kicks off her shoes and wobbles into the sitting room off the foyer. Em had decorated everything. But this was the room she loved the most. It feels like the right place to bring her back to consciousness.

Teagan begins to power on the Em-in-the-Eye, then stops. *This is a special occasion. Em deserves a throne.*

Teagan grabs a rose-colored pillow from a side chair and throws it onto a gold-upholstered loveseat. It bounces off the seat and onto the floor. She winces. *Too rough.*

She drops Em-in-the-Eye on the floor and jogs over to the pillow. She is about to grab it when she realizes what she's done. She runs back to the sleeping orb. "Oh! I'm sorry," she apologizes to Em-in-the-Eye. "That was disrespectful. But you'll love what I'm making for you. I promise."

She fluffs the pillow and places it in the center of the loveseat. Pivoting carefully, she retrieves Em-in-the-Eye and arranges her 'face-out' on the rosy pillow. Pleased with the tableau, Teagan boots Em-in-the-Eye up. "There, your highness." She sits on the floor.

Lights blink across the face of the orb. The voice is Em's even if the face is not. "Teagan?"

Teagan masks a shiver with a smile. "Hi, Em. Welcome home!"

The lights along the face of the Eye don't change much as Em responds, "Thanks. What time is it? Or should I ask what day it is?" The orb is glowing a faint rose-gold.

This will take some getting used to: hearing her wife's voice coming out of the Eye's speakers. The tone is even, but Teagan can't help reading her wife's impatience into it. "Same day. Nine-thirty. At night."

"Well, it couldn't be morning, you uploaded me at ten a.m."

This is just an observation, Teagan reminds herself. *It's not a dig.* But that doesn't stop Em's words from hurting. "That's right. How are you feeling?" As soon as Teagan says it, she wishes she could take it back. *Dummy. She can't feel anything.*

Instead of shooting back a response, Em-in-the-Eye cackles. It's mirthless laughter, but something the living Em would have done.

Teagan relaxes. NeuroNet made a good connection: ridiculous statements should trigger laughter. *It's not personal, these comments. I don't have to take them personally. I can't hurt Em's feelings anymore. And she's not trying to hurt mine.*

It's liberating: this idea that Em's state of being is neutral. Almost like a pet. *I can project what I think she's feeling,* Teagan thinks, *but that doesn't mean it's real.*

The household Eye enters the sitting room. "Incoming call from Dr. Tito Ngata," it intones.

"Oh, look, it's my twin," Em-in-the-Eye cracks. She wobbles a bit as she tries to emulate its flight. "Man, it's going to take me some time to master the controls in this thing. It's a lot different than walking."

Teagan can't help smiling. "I'm glad you didn't lose your sense of humor."

"Well, if I had to lose my head, at least the machine let me keep something."

"True." Teagan wants to ask Em if confinement in the Eye is better than being dead. Instead, begs Em's patience. "Sorry. I have to take this call."

Tito's torso appears above the chair. Teagan smiles. "Hey Tito."

"Teagan! How is Em doing?" His glasses bounce in a forehead crease as he smiles.

"Tito!" Em-in-the-Eye responds before Teagan can speak for her. "Tell the police: someone stole my body and stuck me in this tin can!"

Tito's magic eyebrows rise, sending his glasses crashing down. He laughs. "Sounds like you're doing well."

"Teagan just booted me up, so maybe give me a few hours and then ask again," Em says.

"Will do." Tito's eyes dart to Teagan. "Hey, can we talk in private?"

Teagan frowns. "Em?"

"No problem," Em-in-the-Eye says. "I'll slip into something more comfortable." Her orb hovers unsteadily before finding its balance. "Remind me to ask the kitchen Eye for flying lessons."

Teagan waits for Em to ascend to the second level before speaking. "What is it? Something bad?"

Tito looks over his shoulder, a nervous tic. "Investors are calling for an emergency meeting tomorrow. You, me, and Carter need to get on the same page first."

Uh-oh. "What time is the meeting?"

"Ten a.m."

Teagan's mind begins to whirl. "Tell Carter to meet us at eight in the Executive Suite. Bring whatever dashboard data you have."

13

Teagan pivots out of the driver's seat. With shock, she registers Tito and Carter's figures silhouetted by the Executive Suite door. She tries not to sound testy as she says, "I'm early. What are you doing here already?"

"We never left," Tito explains.

Carter still hasn't shaved. "Glad you're here. We need to get started." He and Tito head inside.

"Hey!" Teagan runs after them. "Aren't you going to ask if I want coffee or to use the restroom first?"

The Executive Suite Eye hands her a mug of black coffee. Teagan thanks it. Now that Teagan is looking at Tito in the bright office lights, she can see the skin beneath his eyes looks thin and dry. Carter is still wearing the clothes he had on at dinner. It's clear neither of them slept. "Why didn't you tell me to come in when you called?"

"It was your first night home with Em," Carter said. "You told Tito you'd be in at eight . . ."

Teagan's brows knit. "It's not like Em has a body, so I wasn't getting lucky or anything. If I'd known you were here, I would have come in, too."

Tito waves her concern away. "It doesn't matter. You're here now. You remember me telling you about the suicide in Chicago?"

Teagan nods. "The El train."

"Yes. His name was Jethro Bolan." Tito flicks an image from the corner of the screen to its heart, where it enlarges. The vid runs on a ten-second loop. The train is arriving. The loved one looks at it and then steps onto the tracks. The train makes contact. The android's shell blows apart, pelting people on the platform waiting for the train.

Teagan flinches. "Jesus." The sound is off, but Teagan can see the horrified faces of the bystanders. She wishes she couldn't. "Was anyone hurt?"

"Yes." But by the way Carter says it, Teagan can tell that's not the part he cares about. "This is what the investors want to discuss."

"Of course, they do." The clip is playing again. Teagan closes her eyes. "Can we turn that off?"

Tito pinches the image and slides it to the edge of the frame. He grabs another image—this one a map—and centers it. There's a red pin over Atlanta and one over Chicago.

"Dee in Atlanta and Jethro in Chicago?" Teagan waits for both of her boys to nod. "Dee was bipolar. Is that something Jethro also suffered from?"

"No." Tito pulls up Jethro's dashboard. "No history of mental illness. No documented suicide attempts when he was alive."

"Which doesn't mean he didn't try, just that no one told anyone," Teagan points out.

Carter nods. "And we did find something in the post-upload autopsy report."

He's pacing. That always makes Teagan nervous. She leans forward. "Well . . . What did you find?"

Tito's eyes dart to Carter before he goes on. Teagan hates it when he does that. It makes her feel like they're keeping secrets or don't trust her. Tito clears his throat. "He was on the verge of liver failure brought on by acute cirrhosis."

She frowns. "That's not a mental disease. Jethro was an alcoholic?"

"Theoretically," Tito says. "We haven't confirmed with his guardian, but that's what it looks like."

Teagan sighs. "So, what's the connection?"

Carter stops pacing. "That's what we've spent all night trying to figure out. I was hoping you'd see something we can't."

"Okay." *He really looks like shit.* "You should really shave before the investor meeting," she tells him. Carter's mouth forms a thin white line of frustration. Teagan holds up her hands to calm him down. "I'm thinking! But I had to say that before I forgot. It won't make the investors feel any better if it looks like you've been up all night. Even if you have been."

Carter looks to Tito to defend him, but Tito looks like a warmed over turd, too. Teagan can't help laughing. "Seriously, we have a shower in this suite. You both need to use it before we go down. I hope you have a spare suit or something in your offices."

While the boys seethe, Teagan's mind works the problem. She thinks about the alcoholics she knows. "Why do people drink?" *What do they have in common with someone with bipolar disorder?*

Carter stiffens. "Are you asking me?"

"I wasn't thinking of you specifically," Teagan lies. "Why do people drink?"

"To celebrate something?" Tito says so earnestly, Teagan is reminded that he almost never touches the stuff.

"Sometimes. But I'm thinking more of people who drink to excess. Alcoholics. Why do they drink?"

"My Dad drank because he couldn't deal with real life," Carter says.

Teagan nods. "And what was it about life that he was trying to escape?"

"His own grief . . . and depression."

Teagan wonders if Carter realizes how much he and his father have in common. "Depression—I think that's the link."

Tito crosses his beefy arms across his broad chest. "Not everyone who's depressed attempts suicide—"

"—and not everyone who attempts suicide wants to die. I know," Teagan says.

Carter's brow furrows. "I still don't know if we can conclusively call what happened to Dee a suicide."

Teagan frowns. "No, but the investors will want us to have thought through what it means if she was."

Tito pulls up the statistics. "Okay, so two-thirds of the people who commit suicide were depressed at the time, but among the population of the clinically depressed, only three to five percent attempt suicide."

"That's good," Carter says. "We can remind investors not to confuse correlation with causation."

Tito nods. "And there's the question Teagan brought up on *Humanity Now*: why would someone given the gift of eternal life want to kill themselves?"

"Remember: we're not talking about someone," Teagan says. "Loved ones aren't people, they're androids. They can't feel. They can't want. They exist. We gated the AI specifically so they wouldn't change. So how could they develop anything? Much less depression? That doesn't make any sense."

Carter stops pacing. His face lights up. "You're right. If they weren't suicidal prior to uploading, how would they develop that impulse?"

"And if that impulse is a rare one . . ." Tito lets that thought trail off.

"So, we're in agreement?" Teagan waits for each of them to nod. "Good. I'm glad I didn't lose any sleep over this." She can't resist rubbing it in. "See? You didn't need me before eight a.m. I solved this in—" she checks the monitor's clock. "—thirty minutes."

Tito rubs his head. "That doesn't explain what did happen, though. Why did Jethro step in front of the El train? Why did Dee jump off the Civic Center platform?"

Carter waves his hand impatiently. "We don't know for a fact that Dee jumped."

"True," Teagan admits. "And lots of people cross the El track to get to the uptown platform. Maybe that was Jethro's intention and he got stuck or distracted. Is that possible?"

Tito chews his lip in thought before admitting, "It is."

"That would be a glitch. Would a glitch show up on his dashboard?" Teagan asks.

"Not necessarily." Tito scrolls to Jethro's last few hours. On the graph, they form a normal looking series of arcs. "There's no cognitive spikes denoting a distressing thought or impulse."

"And suicide has to be the most distressing thought there is," Carter adds.

"I think we have our story, boys." Teagan smiles broadly. "At this point, we're investigating potential glitches, but from the evidence we have, there's nothing to worry about."

14

As they step into the elevator, Carter takes Teagan's hand and squeezes it. "Thank you."

She laughs. "For what?"

"For always making things better." Freshly shaved, showered and in a clean suit, Carter looks a decade younger than he did when she arrived this morning.

Tito chuckles. "I don't know, I think we would have arrived at the same conclusion eventually."

"Right," Teagan cracks. "After your second sleepless night and third nervous breakdown."

"I don't think they call them 'nervous breakdowns' anymore," Carter says with a straight face.

Teagan nods. Names for things change all the time. It's something of a running joke for their generation, although they are sensitive to why they need to be sensitive. "What do they call them?"

"A symptom of mental disorder," Tito says. "It's no longer its own 'thing.'"

"Can I still say, 'panic attack?'"

"Yeah," Carter says. "And for the record: I had four of those last night. I probably would have had an easy dozen if you hadn't come in this morning to rescue us."

Teagan cracks her knuckles like a fixer in an old gangster movie. "What would you boys do without me?"

"I don't think either of us wants to find out," Tito says, and he sounds like he means it.

The elevator arrives on the main conference room floor. Carter leads them out. Teagan smiles at Tito, to thank him for his unexpected sweetness, and nearly crashes into Carter's back. She gives him a playful whack. "Why'd you stop walking?"

Carter's fists clench. "What is she doing here?" he growls.

Teagan peers around him and sighs. *Aya Wakahisa.* "I don't know. I didn't invite her." Teagan tenses. She's glad to see Aya. They need her help. But they have enough to deal with this morning. *Maybe she'll wait until after we're done with the investors?*

Aya brushes her long, dark hair over one narrow shoulder and approaches Carter, hand extended. "Good morning." Carter just stares at her hand. She withdraws it. "I take it Tito did not tell you I would be here?"

The blood rises in Carter's cheeks. "No."

Teagan is glad she's not Tito. She's almost afraid to look at him. Carter's glare could melt steel.

Tito blushes and stammers, "We've been so busy, I totally forgot."

"No matter," Teagan says, stepping in to relieve some of the tension. "You can tell us now. Why are you here?"

"This is a meeting for the investors, is it not?" Aya smiles. "Tito mentioned you were having difficulty raising the gap in funds you need. So . . . here we are."

Teagan struggles to maintain her composure. "You're . . . filling the gap?"

Aya nods.

Teagan's eyebrows shoot up. "Investing everything we need?"

Aya smiles and nods again.

Teagan wants to cheer. They need Aya's money. *And if she's deeply invested, she'll want to consult!* They need Aya's mind back on the team . . . Teagan wants to scream, *Thank you, Tito!* and give him a huge hug. But the look on Carter's face stops her. This is the best case scenario, but who knows how long it will take Carter to see it. In the meantime, Teagan doesn't want him to think she doesn't have his back. He's already so close to losing it. She restrains the urge to whoop, and instead says, "How generous of you. Tito, you'll have to catch us up on the details after the meeting."

Ignoring the disappointed look on Aya's face, Teagan steers Carter toward the boardroom. The glass doors swing open as they approach. Near the top, the glass is clear, which gives this room an illusion of openness. But at a strategic point, the panes appear frosted. This obscures the faces of anyone seated from people passing by outside. The soundproofing in this room is excellent, too. From the outside, looking in, you cannot penetrate the conversation or gain any context. This is Teagan's design. Carter and Tito didn't see the point at first. But she's sure they're grateful for it now. Carter could scream his head off and no one on the support staff would know. If anything leaks to *Humanity Now*, they'll know the leak had to come from inside this room.

Teagan scans the faces around the table. She can tell they're tense because no one's standing around schmoozing. They're all sitting in various states of anxious anticipation, waiting for them to start the meeting. There's still fifteen minutes to go. It's eerie being in a room full of money guys with no one talking. She takes the head seat. Tito takes the seat on the left. Carter sits to her right. *I can't sit here for the next fifteen minutes like this.* Teagan clears her throat. "I think we're all here. Should we start early, then?"

Ignoring the panicked look on Carter's face, Teagan focuses on the half-dozen men in front of her. She knows other tech titans like being on a first-name basis with their stakeholders. But she likes to keep them at arm's length. There's something about the formality of calling them by their last names that helps her feel in control. That's handy, especially since they're usually chomping at the bit to have her, Carter, or Tito make some major about-face on policy or tech—neither of which they understand.

Aya moves to the head seat at the opposite end of the table. "I think that is a good idea."

Mr. Gransden, whose family is one of Peachtree Battle's old guards, sits up a little straighter. "Who's this?" His outrage is so sincere, Teagan bites the inside of her cheek to keep from laughing.

"Gentlemen, Dr. Aya Wakahisa has generously closed the funding gap we needed to launch our IPO."

A murmur of approval sweeps the sea of old, wrinkled, white, money men. The only reason why they give NeuroNet money is to watch it grow. It can't grow without an IPO. And IPO means they might make their investment money back plus interest. This is good news. Sexy news. *If someone is willing to put money in,* she can almost hear them thinking, *then nothing they see on TV can be that bad.*

Teagan doesn't have to look at Carter. She can feel him relax. Hitting the fundraising goal after struggling for so long must feel good. Especially since he lost investors after Dee's incident. *I hope that's enough of an olive branch to forgive Aya.*

Mr. Delaney, who owns most of the land west of the downtown connector raises his hand. Teagan likes it when they're deferential. She gives him permission to speak. "That was a significant gap . . . ."

"It was," Aya says in a distinctly no-shit-Sherlock way. "But I helped build this company. And it would be a shame for it not to grow and reach its full potential."

Mr. LeClerk, who had one brilliant billion-dollar idea twenty years ago, clears his throat. "Does that mean . . ."

"That I am the majority shareholder?" Aya cuts in. "Yes. Yes, it does."

Teagan imagines she can hear the men shriveling in their seats as they realize their influence is dwindling. Aya exudes Big Dyke Energy as she basks in their dawning awareness. For the first time, Teagan regrets uploading Em. *If I were free . . .* She dismisses the thought. It's bad enough to screw with your friends. Fucking a shareholder would be a new kind of low.

As much as Teagan enjoys watching the men squirm, it's not why they're here. She clears her throat to draw their focus. "Last week, a loved one fell in front of a MARTA train. This week, a similar incident appeared to take place in Chicago." The men settle. "As you know, at the core of NeuroNet is the promise that your loved ones never really have to die. The idea that they might cut short this gift of eternal life is extremely upsetting. That's why I want to assure you that is not what is happening."

Mr. Picot, on break from the Georgia legislature, raises a neatly cuffed arm. "Then what is happening, Dr. McKenna?"

"Tito, bring up the dashboards for Jethro Bolan and Dee Claybourne, please."

Tito's heavily muscled frame moves with alarming dexterity. He spreads his hands, and the screen jumps to life between them, two graphs betraying no spikes or swells, as even as a lazy river. "As you can see, these charts plot the neural activity of the uploads. This is how we stress-test the units and how we monitor them for potential issues."

He pulls up a third chart. This one looks dangerously sharp and chaotic. "This is from our friends at the National Institute for Health. It's the neural activity of a suicidal person. You see how the activity appears to hover above this line? The two uploads in question never reach cognitive distress anywhere near these levels."

Teagan nods her approval and Tito sits, leaving the images up for the investors. They don't understand much, but data—especially in pictorial form—holds more sway than words. "We know the data doesn't support the bot suicide narrative." She lets that land. "Carter, would you like to share what we discovered from an engineering standpoint?"

Carter jumps a little. Teagan kicks herself for not warming him up better. *But he should have expected me to pass the ball to him.* They always strive to appear as a united front at these meetings, sharing the burden of presenting. When the news is financial, Carter runs point. When the update is technological in nature, Tito leads the meeting. And when things are in crisis, that's when the boys lean on her to keep things on track.

Thankfully, Carter recovers quickly. She surveys the room. *I may have been the only one who noticed.* Still, she feels tense. *Something is deeply wrong with him.* She makes a mental note to corner him later. He's better than most men about expressing himself. But he's obviously holding something in that he needs to share.

"One of the major developmental decisions we had to make early on at NeuroNet regarded the operating system," Carter begins. "As you might remember, we rely on an artificial intelligence-powered operating system to make the connection between batches of extracted life data the way the brain naturally does between its neural networks to generate responses." Teagan notices he's pointedly avoiding looking at Aya.

"When you work with artificial intelligence, you're basically programming a beginning point and then setting it loose," he continues. "If you gate it, then it spirals inside the same parameters you've set. It works with the initial data set—in our case, the uploaded consciousness of the loved one—without elaborating on it. As time goes on, the system becomes more efficient at processing data inputs and formulating appropriate responses. This consistency means that the person you upload today will still look and act the same twenty years from now—no surprises."

Carter finally glances at Aya. "That's why we gate our uploads. If you don't gate them, and let the AI run wild, then you cannot predict who your loved one will become."

He smiles at the men. "As you can imagine, were we to ungate the AI that powers the NeuroNet operating system, it would cause evolutionary growth that would warp our original intent. Your loved one would be familiar to you after the upload. But eventually, as the ungated AI evolved to evoke responses with greater efficiency and began to include new datasets, your loved one would start surprising you with their words and actions. They would continue to 'evolve' until they were no longer recognizable to their guardians or former family. In this scenario, I could see suicidal or even homicidal impulses appear. But we did not program our loved ones to evolve. Therefore, it's impossible that they would develop such impulses on their own."

Aya smiles. Her voice is soft and low. "I suggest that we ungate a unit and see if they will."

Carter makes a choking sound. "I'm sorry, were you listening? I just explained why we shouldn't do that."

"I was." Aya looks so cool that Teagan doesn't know if she wants to kiss or slap her. "And it seems to me that you are missing something."

Carter folds his arms in front of him. "And that would be . . . ?"

Aya taps a slender finger against the table. "How are you currently testing the units?"

Carter darts a glance at Teagan. She can read his unspoken thought: *Should we tell them about the surveillance we're doing?* If Carter shares the news, Teagan knows how it will sound. He's not a gifted extempore speaker.

She jumps on that sword. "There are always other explanations, other possibilities that must be explored and tested to eliminate potential risks. In one of the scenarios we've investigated, we asked, 'What would happen if a pre-existing personality trait, habit, or activity could trigger suicidal behavior?' In theory, if a person were suicidal before being uploaded or had attempted the act—say when they were a teenager—then it would exist in the NeuroNet along with everything else from that person's consciousness. And if it exists in the NeuroNet, then it would not have to be 'learned.' It might emerge one day as an action the bot takes in response to stimuli."

Aya purses her lips. "That did not answer my question."

"I'm not finished," Teagan says, annoyed. "As you all know, my wife recently was uploaded. She has a history of mental illness, and her diagnosis was the same as Dee Claybourne's." Teagan ignores the noises the men are making. "Carter, Tito, and I still believe very strongly that there's no reason why a loved one—being given the gift of eternal life—would waste it. But just in case, we are closely observing my wife's dashboard for clues to see if that kind of behavior may develop so that we can understand how to prevent it from happening to anyone else."

Aya's eyes narrow. "How many other bots are you observing in this way?"

Teagan is unsure how to answer this. She looks at Tito for help.

"We have isolated twenty potential risk factors," Tito says. "We have as many units undergoing the same tests."

Teagan holds her breath, waiting for one of the men to ask if they have consent from the guardians. She can feel sweat collecting underneath her bra. She doesn't want to lie, but she's prepared to if it means ending this line of questioning.

Aya is the first to speak. "Can we clone the uploads and run simultaneous stress tests with ungated systems?"

Mr. LeClerk sighs audibly.

Teagan smiles. *Thank God, they're bored and ready to move on.* "Dr. Wakahisa, let's continue this conversation offline. Meet us in the Executive Suite after this meeting."

Mr. LeClerk motions to adjourn if there are no further questions. Mr. Picot seconds the motion. Aya follows Tito, Carter and Teagan into the elevator. It's a long, icy, silent ride to the top. But as soon as the elevator doors to the Executive Suite close behind them, Carter wheels around, face purple with rage. "What the fuck, Aya?"

Aya sets her purse on the fluffy marshmallow-like couch and sits down. "I live to serve," she says dryly. "You are welcome, by the way."

Tito steps between Aya and Carter and places his hands on Carter's shirt. "It's my fault. I should have told you Aya wanted to help us close the gap and figure out potential solutions."

Carter's mouth moves, but no sound escapes.

Teagan says what she knows he must be thinking, "I thought Aya was here as an investor."

"My investment is conditional on being part of your solutions team." Aya adjusts the lacy cuffs of her shirt with birdlike fingers. "If you bar my involvement, my money walks with me."

Teagan and Tito look at Carter. *Please say yes,* Teagan thinks at him. *I know you hate her, but we need her help.*

"We need the money," Tito reminds him.

"No fucking way," Carter says.

Aya laughs.

Carter tries to step around Tito, without success.

"Carter," Teagan warns him. She doesn't think he's capable of violence, but Aya's always provoked him to do unpredictable things.

Aya gets up slowly. "When you get over the shock, let me know your final answer."

"That is my final answer," Carter spits out.

Aya laughs again. "Ask your Eye what happened in Baltimore this morning. Then let me know if you still feel the same."

Teagan's spine freezes. "What happened in Baltimore?" But her words bounce off Aya's back. She asks the boys, "What happened in Baltimore?" Their eyes are as wide and clueless as her own. "Eye! Search the web for 'NeuroNet, Baltimore.'"

The suite's Eye hovers over to them. "I've found three results for 'NeuroNet, Baltimore': article, video, and radio. Which would you prefer?"

Teagan can barely get the words out; her mouth is so dry. "Video, please."

The Eye rotates to project against the nearest vertical surface. Roz Able's face appears and Teagan's heart sinks. The *Humanity Now* reporter tees up her story, "This is Roz Able on the scene of what appears to be yet another NeuroNet suicide."

Teagan can't breathe. Her fingers work to undo the buttons at her neck. Beside her, Tito whistles softly.

Carter gasps. "Shit. Shit. Shit."

15

Teagan knows there's no great time to transfer Em into her new body. Still, she wishes it wasn't today. She promised Em a second honeymoon. But Teagan doesn't see how the boys will survive without her.

Since the Baltimore incident, media inquiries have come in daily. The threat of another android suicide looms over them like a digital sword of Damocles. But Carter insists he and Tito will be okay.

"It's only ten business days," Carter had said. "One of us should get a break."

Maybe while I'm on this 'honeymoon,' they'll bring in some new blood, Teagan hopes. *Or Carter will admit we need Aya's help.*

Without Aya, NeuroNet is an echo chamber. There are only so many different approaches she, Carter and Tito can generate on their own. *And we're exhausted. We need new eyes on this situation.*

Teagan's hand cramps. She loosens her grip on the bouquet she's bought to give the new and improved Em. Flowers always make Teagan feel like she's apologizing for something. When she and Em lived off Memorial Drive, Teagan wondered if the teddy bear and rose vendors had any clientele other than cheating spouses. *Who needs to buy flowers before going home?* Surely no one with a clean conscious. Yet, here she is, a bouquet of peonies in hand, standing in Bay Four, waiting for her wife to 'wake up' in her new body.

"Transfer is complete," Tito says. "Upload is rendering."

Teagan breathes into the knot of anxiety in her chest, mentally undoing it. *This is good,* she tells herself. Although she will miss Em-in-the-Eye floating around behind her, cracking jokes. It reminds Teagan of when they were friends in high school. Back when words and wit were enough to entangle and entice. Before the mess of bodies and feelings entered the equation. When being there was enough.

Em's an upload. She's not going to have taxing emotional or physical demands, Teagan reassures herself. *Besides this is a happy occasion. A new start.*

Teagan's booked a week at The Grove Park Inn. It's where they honeymooned the first time. It seems fitting they go back now.

She asks Tito, "Are you sure you'll be okay when I'm gone?"

Tito smiles. "Of course. There haven't been any incidents since Baltimore. There's no reason to stay."

Teagan laughs. "I was kind of hoping you'd ask me not to go."

"You promised Em, right?"

"I did." But she really doesn't want to leave. "If you need me . . ."

Tito narrows his eyes. "Carter and I should be able to last two weeks without you."

But can I spend two weeks alone with Em, without you two? Teagan thinks about the Baltimore incident. That bot wasn't an alcoholic, wasn't bipolar, wasn't anything they could track down in any documents. A complete tabula rasa. "Any new variables?"

"I've been up and down the records. Nothing new."

Teagan closes her eyes. "What about our surveillance set? Any insights there?"

"No. But I talked with Aya—"

Teagan cuts him off. This is news. "Does Carter know?"

Tito blushes.

Her pulse races with excitement. But she warns, "Until he gives the okay, you shouldn't be talking with her."

"I know . . ."

Em stirs. Teagan nearly drops the peonies. She touches the cool metal of the surgical bed. "Hey . . ."

Em's eyes flicker open. "Teagan?"

Teagan smiles. "Hey honey. How are you feeling?"

Em blinks and frowns. She stares at Teagan for a long time before finally saying, "You're kidding, right?"

"That's what I love about you." Teagan covers Em's face with kisses. "Your sense of humor."

"Well, now there's more of me to love," Em says, eyes twinkling. She stretches her arms and wiggles her toes. "God, it feels good to be back in a body again."

16

In the car, Em rests a hand on Teagan's thigh. It's unsettling. *When was the last time Em reached for me?* A twinge of something like hope flutters inside Teagan's rib cage.

Teagan never stopped desiring Em. *But there's only so many times you can get rejected before you stop trying.* When Em did initiate sex, it turned out that it was because she wanted something—to be uploaded or have money added to her account, or, or, or . . . *But it didn't always used to be that way.*

Teagan pats Em's hand. It feels warm and real. In the amber light of magic hour, Em looks healthy, vital.

I've never stopped loving her, Teagan realizes. Teagan hooks a hand around Em's neck and cranes toward her. It's risky, taking her eyes off the route, but she wants a kiss.

The car beeps angrily at her shifting weight. Em laughs and pushes her away, playfully saying, "I think you need to get back in your seat, driver."

Teagan smiles. *She didn't reject me; she's only teasing.* This is a good sign. "What good is autopilot if I can't kiss my wife?"

Em's eyes widen in mock shock. "Don't tell me Dr. McKenna is thinking about breaking the rules?"

"I don't have to tell you. I'll show you." Teagan lunges across the gap between their seats, invoking the car's ire once again. Kissing Em isn't as awkward as it could be. Of course, the angle makes full contact difficult. The car's alarms impede Teagan's desire to fully relax into the kiss. But

Em's lips and body respond. That alone is thrilling. But then Teagan's mind fast-forwards to the bedroom. *I don't know if I'm ready for that.*

Em pulls away. "What's wrong? Did you get a gear in your teeth?"

"Nothing's wrong," Teagan lies. "I didn't want to wreck the car before we got to the hotel." She grins in what she hopes is a winning way. "You know, I asked Tito what sex with a bot would be like—"

Em howls. "You asked Tito to tell you about sex?"

Teagan laughs despite herself. "He's got more experience than any of us with the Model Two bodies. Carter and I were both married when we needed to test the sex functions. He volunteered—"

"Because he's a creeper—"

"Because he's a scientist," Teagan corrects. "And . . . he's not creepy. He is socially challenged."

Em lays her head back against the passenger seat headrest in a very Em way. Teagan marvels, *That's damn good programming.*

Em turns slightly toward her. Her amber eyes glitter mischievously. Teagan wonders, *Is mischief driven by intellect? I thought it was fueled by emotion. Em's clearly expressing playful feelings.*

A thought occurs: *What else is in there that I thought got left behind?* The possibilities of discovery are exciting.

Em smiles. "Penny for your thoughts?"

Teagan considers how much she wants to share. "I was thinking about how much I'm enjoying your companionship. Becoming a loved one didn't rob you of much of you at all."

Em cocks her head in thought, another very 'Em' gesture. "I don't know if I'd go so far as to say that," she says. "Could you still say that I'm human?"

"You've all your core memories. You move and act as you did when you were alive. You are still my wife." Teagan swallows the lump forming in her throat. This is difficult to say, but she feels she must. "I still desire you . . ."

Em curls her legs up under her. The soft golden light shaves years off her face. She looks like the girl Teagan fell in love with. Em traces a pattern over Teagan's thigh with a slender finger. "You've always loved smart girls."

Teagan blushes. "I have." *Is Em being ironic? She's smart, but she's not in the same league as Aya.*

For years, Em lobbied to open their marriage, waving Aya as a carrot to tempt Teagan. But Teagan resisted. It didn't feel right to share herself or her wife with anyone else. Not that Em respected the same rules. *But she's all mine now.*

Em is extending an olive branch. Her fingers are in Teagan's lap. *I don't care if this is real or not,* Teagan thinks. *I deserve this.* She unclenches her legs. *The automatic pilot should keep the car upright. I can play a little.* She lets her legs widen into a V. Em's fingers dance, and Teagan involuntarily jerks them together. "Sorry! It tickles."

"I can do better than tickle." Em smirks. "Lay back and let me treat you." She unfastens the button on Teagan's pants. "As long as I stay in my seat, the car won't yell at us, right?"

"Right." Teagan's throat tightens. *Why are you so anxious? Just enjoy yourself.* She breathes deeply, trying to relax. It's disorienting, knowing that she's being loved by a machine.

Not a machine, your loved one. Em's fingers know what to do, and that makes it easier for Teagan to give in. It's hot, being touched this way. And the edge of knowing that they're doing something dangerous makes it even sexier. With gratitude, Teagan lets the pressure mount, break, and roll over her in a blissful wave. "Oh . . . *Thank you.*" She wants to enjoy this feeling, hold on to it, stay in it, but she hears Em complain: "I can't smell anything."

Teagan asks, "What do you mean you can't smell anything?"

Em holds up her fingers. "I wanted to smell you." She licks one. "Or taste you."

Tenderness replaces annoyance. "Did you enjoy yourself?"

Em bites her lip, something she would have done while alive, and Teagan's heart leaps at the engineering marvel. After a moment, Em says, "I enjoyed watching you enjoy yourself."

"Were you always a voyeur?" Teagan remembers Em being more selfish in the bedroom. "I always thought you were more of a pillow princess."

"I don't mind watching." A sly grin creeps across her face. "But I'm hoping I get to be a more active participant once you get me in the bedroom."

Teagan matches the smile although the thought of fully engaged sex fails to ignite the same anticipation. She buttons up her pants. "We'll be there soon." The car is descending. She doesn't want the hotel valet to see her half-dressed.

"Yes, please." Em smiles. "I can't wait to get you alone."

Teagan's smile feels frozen. She lies, "I think I'm going to like our second honeymoon."

Em laughs. "Well, anything would be better than our first."

"What was wrong with our first?" Teagan searches her memories. "We always fought, but I don't see . . ."

"We fought the whole time!" Em shakes her head as if to dislodge the memory. "I thought you were going to divorce me."

"What were we fighting about?" The fog is lifting somewhat. Teagan remembers being upset, but the cause is still hazy.

"The bartender." Em laughs. "You really don't remember?"

Teagan's brows knit. "He was hitting on you?" It's a good guess. Everyone hit on Em. Even after Em lost her hair, she still turned heads.

Em shakes with laughter. "He propositioned me!"

"And we fought about that?"

"No," Em says. "We fought about whether or not it would count as an infidelity if I slept with a man versus a woman."

The car bumps down on the landing pad. Teagan unfastens her seatbelt and pops the trunk. She wants to get out before the valet gets there so she can grab their bags. "If we're married and you sleep with someone else, I don't see how that isn't an infidelity."

"But if it's just sex," Em says, "and you're the one I love, then it doesn't count. I'm just getting something I need that you couldn't give me."

The air grows heavy. Teagan buries her head in the trunk. *God, why is she mentioning this again?* They have too many bags for Teagan to carry comfortably, but she waves off the valet. She stumbles inside. Em calls out for her to slow down and wait, but Teagan pretends not to hear. She shuffles uncomfortably toward the elevator.

Em catches her there. "You know, the valet would have been happy to help you."

Teagan knows she's right, but she won't set the bags down. Even though they're cutting off the circulation in each shoulder. "We have money because I don't let people do things for me that I can do for myself."

Em laughs. "So stubborn. But you're no longer young. You better watch it or you're going to stroke out."

Teagan frowns. "I'm not even fifty yet."

Em smiles. "I'm never going to be fifty."

A frigid river sweeps over Teagan's temples and pools around the nape of her neck. *It's true. We've shared our last milestone.* From now on, Em will remain forty-seven as Teagan continues to age. She thinks of the portrait wall in Carter's house. Her stomach twists. Em's bright smile only makes her feel worse. *Do other guardians get buyer's remorse? Or is there something wrong with me?*

The elevator doors clang shut. It's a short ride to the second floor. The bags are digging into Teagan's shoulders, but maybe she deserves the pain. What was fun in the car is too real now. *I let her pleasure me. I'm going to have to reciprocate. What if I can't?* There's a sleep function she can activate by pressing on Em's eyelids. *But there's no subtle way to do that.* She tries to recapture the desire she felt only moments ago. *What are you freaking out about? People have sex with Model Two androids all the time. Hell, people even pay to have sex with the empty bots. This one is filled with a person you love.*

Teagan tries to blot out the contrary voice that wants to argue whether this relationship is loving. *I owe it to both of us to make a fresh start. Em's different now.*

Em dances in front of her, down the hallway. She opens the hotel room door and poses coquettishly. Her exuberance makes Teagan feel worse because the closer they come to the bedroom, the less capable she feels of making love to Em. Teagan stumbles into the room, bouncing off one of the narrow hallway walls. The room is brightly lit and cozy, a couch and sitting area to the left with a door leading to the bedroom and bathroom to the right.

She dumps the bags on the bed.

"Hey!" Em laughs and pulls a luggage caddy out of the closet. "Not on the bed! We're going to need space."

"Sorry," Teagan says, but she wants to apologize for so much more. *At least we may get some useable data from this experiment, even if I terminate it early.*

Em saunters up and throws her arms around Teagan's neck. She kisses Teagan's cheek. Teagan smiles and squirms out from under Em's grasp. "Sorry, I need to check my phone." It's not a lie, she hasn't checked in with Carter or Tito since they got on the road. "What if they need me?"

Em sits on the bed, folding her arms over her skinny chest. "Is it going to be like this the whole time? This is our honeymoon." She lifts a hand to the neck of her blouse and tugs at a ribbon. The front of her blouse falls open.

Teagan feels desire's sharp bite. *She's so beautiful* . . . "Maybe I don't need to hurry?" She caresses Em's breast.

Em's eyes close to focus on the sensations rippling through her. "I haven't had a body for three months. I want to see what this thing can do." She hooks a finger through the belt loop of Teagan's pants and pulls her close.

A jolt of electricity moves up Teagan's spine. Before she can think of all the reasons why she shouldn't, she is kissing Em. And it feels so real, all hesitation and fear slip away.

17

Teagan bites into the steak with gusto. "I'm starving." She smiles up at Em. "You gave me quite a workout." She expects a sly smile from her lover, a measure of encouragement, a flirtatious response.

Instead, Em curls her lip. "Ew. Workout? How romantic."

"I'm sorry," Teagan backpedals. She lowers her voice to a whisper. "I should have said 'lovemaking.'" She desperately wants Em to understand how important their exchange was. How meaningful.

Em's head tips back and she laughs. "Oh. I forgot what a nerd you are." She sighs and pats Teagan's hand. "I'm glad you enjoyed yourself."

Teagan's brow furrows. "You didn't?" She replays everything. Em seemed engaged. "You didn't feel . . . connected?" *Did I misread her cues? Can a loved one pretend?* "I thought it was fun for you."

Em cocks an eyebrow. "Why? Because I made noise? Women fake orgasms all the time."

"Why would you fake . . .?" Anger and shame washes over Teagan.

"An orgasm?" Em pops a carefully trimmed piece of meat into her mouth. "I always do." She chews and swallows before continuing. "At least, with you, I had to."

That's a lie. She's just trying to upset me, Teagan tells herself. *Although why would an upload go out of its way to be cruel? Isn't that an emotional decision?*

Teagan reconsiders. *Uploads repeat patterns of behavior familiar to them. Maybe she's not trying to be mean, this is just who she is: a cruel bitch.*

Teagan tries to be charitable, but she can't think of anything nice about Em right now. Not hurting like this. *She's always used sex as a bargaining tool. Why would that change?*

Teagan pushes her steak away. She's lost her appetite. She throws her napkin on top of the plate. Dots of blood mar the fabric, but Teagan resists the urge to stop the carnage. She places her elbows on the table and leans forward, practically hissing, "What do you want?"

Em smiles. "Look, thank you for uploading me." She looks so calm Teagan wants to smack her. "But you and I both know we're not a good match." Teagan shakes her head, but Em stops her before she can interrupt. "We have our moments, but you don't make me happy, and I obviously don't make you happy."

"What are you saying?" Teagan's inner critic responds first: *The obvious, dummy. You've thought the same thing a million times.*

Em laughs, shakes her head, and buries her face in her hands. "Jesus, Teagan. The level of denial you're capable of boggles my mind. How can you be so smart but so stupid about people?"

Teagan darts a glance around them. "Can you please lower your voice?" None of the diners are staring yet, but they might if Em's volume increases. "I'll admit, sometimes I'm slow when it comes to interpreting emotional cues. Especially when they're indirect. It's easier for me to deal with facts."

"Oh, I know how you love reducing life to its data points. But shouldn't you be happier now?" The way Em raises her chin hits Teagan as remarkably defiant. "After all, I'm nothing but data now, right?"

"Where is this all coming from?" Teagan makes a mental note to check Em's dashboard after dinner to review with Tito. *Maybe this isn't a spike but a noticeable enough pattern to help us identify if unresolved marital issues might be a potential suicide trigger.* Her cynical inner voice adds, *or homicide.* "Are you asking me for a divorce?"

"No dummy." Em rolls her eyes. "If we divorce, then I get deactivated. Why would I give up the gift of eternal life? I'm not stupid."

Teagan dislikes having her own words thrown back at her. "Then what do you want?"

"My freedom," Em says. "I've been married to you until death us do part. Can we finally try something new?"

Teagan frowns. "You can't move freely around without me. You need to stay within fifty miles of me and my bracelet."

Em shrugs. "Can I invite friends over?

"Why?" Teagan's not sure what else to say.

Em's shoulders sag and she sighs. "I can't believe I'm stuck with you."

Now Teagan can feel people looking. "You don't have to be," she says sharply. "I'll call Tito and Carter and have them deactivate you in the morning." Before Em can respond, Teagan stands and pushes in her chair. "Tell them to charge it to the room."

The dining room is dim enough that she can avoid looking into anyone's face, but Teagan feels the weight of eyes upon her. *This was stupid. I was stupid.* She knows she needs to call Tito and Carter, deactivate Em, and accept this was a horrible mistake. But first, she wants a drink.

There's a small bar area by the grand staircase. Teagan hustles over and orders the signature cocktail. Thank God it's strong because it's almost nauseatingly sweet. The bartender wants to make small talk, but Teagan's not interested. She takes the drink and heads outside. She stands at the top of a long flight of stone steps. Each rough-hewn stone looks like it was hand-cut before being set into the staircase, which matches the stony façade of the historic hotel.

It's amazing that buildings like this exist, Teagan thinks. She spends so much time thinking about the future that being around artifacts that still bear the marks of craftsmanship soothes her. She's standing on at least one hundred and thirty years of history. And who knows how many stories the land underneath these stones could tell her of the millions of years of human existence that came before this hotel was built.

There are footsteps on the stones. "Teagan." Em's voice is gentle, beseeching.

It still annoys Teagan. "Leave me alone."

Em touches Teagan's elbow. "Teagan, I'm . . ."

Teagan steps away from her. "I don't want to talk right now. Go to the room."

Em's face hardens. "Did you already call them?"

"Tito and Carter?" Em nods. "Not yet." *But I will,* Teagan thinks, taking a sip of her overpriced mason jar of sugar water and alcohol.

Em takes a step toward her. "Please, don't."

"Why?"

It almost looks as if tears are gathering in the corners of Em's eyes. *Is that for real?* Teagan wonders if this is one of those ghoulish tricks of Tito's programming: a physiological response triggered by a thought pattern. Once full of importance, now robbed of all emotion and meaning. *What would happen if I said no? Would she really care?* Teagan can't imagine Em truly being affected. *Like a dog you leave when you go to work; they look sad, but they don't really feel anything. Em doesn't feel anything, either. She's not even human anymore. But I'm projecting what she feels on her, like I would on a dog I felt bad about leaving.*

That's what I need to do: leave. Close the door on this horrible chapter and move on.

Em's still looking at her expectantly, but Teagan no longer feels bad about uploading her or guilty that she wants to be free of her now.

"I think, if you look at this rationally from my perspective," Teagan says, "you'll see that it doesn't make any sense to keep you around. If you don't want to be a faithful companion, then deactivating you is the best course of action."

"Is it?" Em's amber eyes reflect gaslit flames from the lamps around them. Her voice is soft, almost a purr. "I exist. I no longer feel. But I think. I respond. I remember what it was like to live. I still want to experience life. I want to experience love. We can do that together. Whether or not I fit your definition of faithful. I can still be a loyal companion, a comfort to you. Even if you can't love me."

The absurdity of Em's logic makes Teagan laugh. "Sex isn't love."

The corner of Em's mouth twitches. "Sex is the foundation of love. And giving it is the greatest gift. Besides, Model Twos dominate sex trade. So, I was made for this. If you can't enjoy it, I know people who will."

Teagan takes another sip, grateful for the lubrication the alcohol is providing. This conversation is not enjoyable, but at least she's not as tense as she'd be sober. She looks out to the steely shadow of the mountains beyond the property's yard.

But Em won't stop talking. "You deserve to be happy, Teagan. This frees you to find other people, too."

A headache is forming. Teagan rubs her eyes and groans. *I'm too tired for this. I'll call Tito and Carter in the morning. They'll probably be surprised the honeymoon lasted this long.* "Drop the line of shit Em. You've always been selfish, and cruel, but this is a new low, even for you. I don't know why I thought you'd be capable of thinking of anyone but yourself."

Em crosses her arms over her sunken chest. "That's rich, coming from you."

Em's a tiny woman. But Teagan doesn't have the strength to push past her. She pivots away from the lobby door and heads down the stairs. *I'll catch the elevator from the ground floor. The door should still be open.*

"Where are you going?" Em calls after her.

Teagan doesn't look back. She needs rest. To be somewhere quiet.

"Teagan, wait." Em grabs at Teagan's elbow.

Teagan tugs, trying to break free. But Em's grip is strong. Stronger than it should be. Teagan yanks again. "This was a mistake. I'll fix it in the morning."

Em pulls Teagan up a half-step. "What do you mean a mistake? What are you going to fix?"

"Go back to the room." Teagan pushes Em's chest, but she still won't let go. "I don't want you here."

"What are you going to fix?" Em shakes her. She speaks to Teagan as if she were a child. "Are you going to fix me? Do you mean you are going to get rid of me?"

Teagan stops struggling. She feels sick. Her head aches. She just wants this to be over. She wants to be sober. She wants to be home, in her bed, with no Em. She opens her eyes. Two Ems are frowning down at her. Teagan forces herself to focus until they are one. "I hate you." She juts her chin out and says, "I don't want you."

"Finally, something we can agree on." Em pushes Teagan away.

Teagan is glad to be free of Em. She raises the glass to her lips, but the liquid misses her mouth. Her mind is confused. The distance between her and Em is growing. But Teagan's feet aren't moving. They aren't even touching the step anymore. She is falling. Teagan's mouth opens in surprise.

Gravity is an efficient beast. With a painful crack, Teagan bounces off a stone with her right hip. The impact sends her flying down over the next few steps. When she lands, it is on her nose. As it twists to kiss her cheek, pain blossoms and spreads from her eyes to her neck.

She keeps twirling, a drunken dancer. She puts out her left arm to stop. But only succeeds in snapping her wrist. Everything hurts. Teagan can't tell if her eyes are open or closed. There is nothing but the searing red and black of pain, it blots out everything but the movement of her body through space. She is suddenly a child, rolling down hills with Carter. The best one was at the far end of the neighborhood lake. The spiky grass hurt so bad, but flying down it was so much fun. She and Carter spend hours laughing their way down the grassy slope.

When they reached the bottom, breathless and nearly broken, they'd lay on their backs until the world stopped spinning, then compete to see who had gotten the best bruises and scrapes.

Teagan wonders if Carter is rolling along behind her. But by the time she reaches the bottom, Teagan is past caring.

18

The beeping won't stop. Teagan opens her eyes, but they are looking at a blank ceiling. She tries to turn her head to widen her view, but it won't budge.

What is happening?

She tries to raise an arm to move her head, but it's trapped in something rigid.

The beeping is so loud. Teagan wants it to stop.

She remembers she has a voice. She uses it. "Can someone turn that off?"

Someone answers her. "Oh, good, you are awake."

Who is that? The voice is familiar.

"I am sorry if that sounds loud," the woman says, "but we need to monitor your vitals. I will see if the nurse can adjust the volume." She moves into Teagan's field of vision. "I wonder why you are so sensitive to that sound?"

Teagan knows who her visitor is now. "Aya? What are you doing here?" That provokes another question. "Where am I?" And better yet, "What happened?"

Aya holds up her hands. "There is only one of me so I hope you do not mind if I answer one question at a time."

The expression on Aya's face makes Teagan laugh.

Aya smiles. "Good. You did not lose your sense of humor. That might come in handy."

That doesn't sound good. "For what?"

"You asked what I am doing here. I am visiting you. In the hospital, to answer your second question."

Hospital? "Why am I in the hospital?" But before she even finishes the sentence, Teagan remembers. "I fell?"

Aya nods. "You did."

Teagan frowns. "Em pushed me away from her . . . Was it an accident? Or . . ."

Aya sits on the narrow bench by the bed. "Unclear. Tito has the hotel security vid in the lab. I am sure he and Carter would be happy to share it with you."

"Have you seen it?" Teagan tries to sit up straighter, but that's not something the cast allows. She will make getting out of this a priority. She has no choice but to relax back against the pillows.

Aya steps closer so Teagan doesn't have to strain to see her. "I have."

Teagan studies Aya's face, but it betrays nothing. "And . . . ?"

Aya waves away Teagan's question with a graceful hand. "It is impossible to tell. You struggled on the steps. She released you. You fell. You almost died. We did not see anything on Em's dashboard to indicate cognitive distress."

"We can ask her." Teagan doesn't relish the idea, but it would be the most efficient solution to find out what happened.

Aya shakes her head. "Your heart stopped. You know the protocol."

Teagan does. "She's gone then?" Aya nods. "Oh." When the guardian's heart stops, their bracelet transmits a kill code to the NeuroNet. That deactivates the connected bot. "I was mad at her. I wanted to deactivate her. I probably would have, if . . . Still . . . I wish I got to say goodbye."

"I am sure you will miss her."

Teagan frowns. "I must be in shock. I don't feel anything."

"They have you on a lot of painkillers." Aya gestures to a bag on a pole. "You broke . . . many things. Too many to name. But nanobots are knitting the bones together. And they work quickly. The doctor says physical therapy can start next week. Maybe, the week after, we can take you home."

"Home . . ." *Home without Em.* It's too final, too large a thought for Teagan to wrap her head around. She thinks about work, instead. "Have there been any more suicides?"

"Not that I have seen," Aya says. "What happened between you and Em . . . Do you think it was an accident?"

"You think she tried to kill me?"

"What if she did?"

Teagan frowns. "That shouldn't be possible."

"By that reasoning, neither is a suicide. Yet, we have seen three." Aya says. "But it clearly is possible. Wishful thinking will not change anything." She leans forward and grips Teagan's hand. "I want to stop NeuroNet androids from developing suicidal intent. And I certainly fear them developing homicidal intent. But it may be too late to stop that from happening."

Teagan tries to sit up. The cast refuses to yield. "What do you mean?"

Aya sighs and pushes a strand of hair away from her face. *She's still so young looking.* Teagan decides to take better care of herself when she gets out of here. Maybe Carter will join her in some kind of exercise program? They're both getting soft and pudgy. She misses the lean strength of her twenties. *It'd be nice to grab any pair of pants in my closet and be able to wear them.* Right now, she must try on two before finding one that fits.

Aya pulls a portable screen from her pocket and unfolds it. Her elegant fingers dance across its surface. It springs to life. The image is clear. It's the interior of a private residence with floor-to-ceiling windows and an old-fashioned piano in one corner. It looks expensive. Not a public space. Those all look grimy.

Teagan squints at the screen since she can't crane her head any closer. "This isn't from a security vid."

"No," Aya confirms.

"Did Carter–"

Aya presses a finger to her own lips, silencing her. Teagan can't crane her head around, but if she could, she's sure she'd see one of the hospital's Eyes hovering nearby. Carter must have hacked the feed somehow. "Is it public knowledge?"

"Not yet," Aya says. "It happened in a jurisdiction friendly to us. We are working with the authorities there to determine a course of action. But–"

Teagan completes her sentence, "Next time we may not be so lucky."

Aya looks pleased. "Exactly. That is why I am hoping there is no 'next time.'"

Teagan focuses on the moving images before her. A woman enters the frame. She is wearing a pink kimono. Her hair is pinned into a chignon. At the base of her neck, Teagan can see one of Tito's tattoos. *She's a loved one.* Tito marks all the NeuroNet models with symbols borrowed from the jade necklaces people wear in New Zealand. It's a twist—the pikorua—symbolizing the bonding of two lives together for infinity.

A teenage girl enters the frame. Her face is swollen and red with tears. The loved one embraces her, but the girl will not be consoled. She pushes the loved one—*her mother*, Teagan thinks—away and disappears. The loved one calls out. A man enters the frame. Teagan asks Aya, "Her husband?"

"Yes."

The audio is hard to hear, but from what Teagan can gather, the husband has done something to upset the child. "He looks familiar. What does he do?"

"Senator."

"Oh," Teagan knows him now. "From Indiana?"

"Yes."

He's been in the news a lot. He's the head of the obstructionist party. He's been pushing for federal mandates to codify transgender fear and hate into federal law. "Is the daughter transgender?"

"Yes, although he does not officially recognize her as a 'she.' He still uses her dead name in press ops."

What a dick, Teagan thinks. The conversation between him and his loved one grows heated. At least, his side of the argument is. She can tell by how red and angry his face is. Spittle flies from his lips. Her face remains impassive. That seems to inflame him. He slaps her. Teagan inhales deeply, expecting the bot to react.

Aya shoots a glance her way. "Keep watching."

The man yells for quite some time, following the loved one around the room as she goes about putting things back into order. "He's awful."

Aya nods. "Many people would agree with you. I think that is one of the reasons why no one has leaked this."

The man stops yelling. He grabs his chest. His face contorts in pain. He falls. He has trouble speaking, but he looks as if he's asking for something. "Aspirin," Aya says. "He is asking for aspirin."

Teagan's father died of a heart attack. She and her mother knew for some time it was a possibility. He ate way too much meat to have healthy arteries. They ran drills to prepare for the worst: give him a baby aspirin, loosen his clothes, and make him comfortable until the medics arrived. Teagan even took a CPR class in case it was needed. The loved one in this vid does nothing to prolong her husband's life. Instead, she kneels by his side, tightens his necktie, and slowly presses on his chest. "That will kill him," Teagan says. "Did she kill him on purpose?"

"Technically, the heart attack is what killed him," Aya says. "But she chose not to help."

The vid flickers out. Teagan can see the sterile hospital wall again. "She didn't try to save him."

Aya folds the screen and fits it back into her pocket. "No, she did not."

"Why do you think that is?"

Aya shrugs. "Perhaps she did not love him."

"But even if she didn't love him, wouldn't she still want to live? Once his heart stops, so would hers, so to speak."

Aya's head tilts and she smiles. "What would you theorize?"

Teagan considers the question. "She is a mother with a distressed child. If the husband is the source of the irritation, she might prioritize the child's needs above his."

Aya nods. "But he is in distress, too. A potentially fatal situation. Would not that concern her?"

"Not if she doesn't love him or had fallen out of love with him before she was uploaded. If there was no love for him in her memory, then the love of the child would be the true allegiance. The child is in pain; the husband is the cause. If the husband dies, he can't cause the child any more pain."

Aya's eyes narrow. "Are you saying she wants him to die?"

"No." Teagan's brows knit, and she glances at the Eye. "The loved ones are input in, input out. There's an efficiency in the way they connect data, thanks to the AI interface. The loved one will solve the problem, using what data is available, in the most efficient way possible. Her child is in pain. She wants to end their suffering. What is the most elegant solution to the problem? Maybe it's to let nature take its course and knock the husband, the irritant, out of the equation."

Aya's laugh rings out, a bell in the sterile room. "Your thoughts are going to some dark places."

"Dark, but honest." Teagan tries to shake her head but finds the medical restraints limiting. "Kids aren't born innocent. They're vicious, selfish, and single-minded. We condition them to be civilized. Even in civilized societies, intelligence can be applied to justify the most heinous crimes. Look at the Nazis and the millions they captured, experimented on, murdered, and then turned into soaps to wash their sins away. Prior to becoming a country of genocidal maniacs, Germany was considered the most enlightened, educated, cultured country in the world."

Aya frowns. "Many former Nazis had no remorse."

"No, because to them, their actions made sense. They were being rational . . . According to the set of facts they drew their conclusions from. You and I look at a distinct set of facts drawn from their actions and can see them for the monsters they were. But I doubt they thought of themselves that way. Similarly, I think that it might be possible for a loved one to do something horrific if it makes sense to them."

"And you think she did not save her husband to help the child?"

"I've never been a mother, and I wasn't close to my own," Teagan says, "but mothers tend to choose what's best for their children over their own needs, right? This is why preserving the life of her husband wasn't a priority."

Aya leans back against the wall. She is a tiny woman. Her knees don't touch the bed the way Teagan's did when she visited Em's bedside. *God, how long ago was that? Could it only be two or three months ago? It feels like years.*

Teagan sighs. "I don't think Em's action was premeditated. She wanted to live. She had to know that if I died, she would, too."

Aya peers at her intently. "So why did she let you fall?"

Teagan stares at her encased body. Not being able to feel her limbs is disorienting. It's almost like an out-of-body experience or a dream. It's not painful, but infinitely unpleasant. "When will they wean me off these painkillers? I don't want to feel like this indefinitely."

"Do not worry about that," Aya says. "You said Em wanted to live. So why do you think she let you fall?"

Teagan purses her lips. "I think she let me fall because it was a better option than putting up with me for the next fifty years."

Aya shakes her head. "Nonsense. You are a phenomenal woman."

Teagan's mouth twists. "I'm a brilliant engineer, a savvy business-person, and a decent scientist. But am I a good human?" She laughs. "I don't know that I have mastered that. I'm a good friend—to Tito and Carter, even you, I hope. But I was a shitty teenager; I argued with my parents and always had to be right. When I grew up, I was an even worse wife: jealous, selfish, obsessed with work, impatient. I'm not an easy person to like."

Aya begins to protest, but Teagan cuts her off. "I'm not upset by it. It's not a new revelation." Teagan smiles. "I loved Em. I did. But I didn't like her most of the time. By the end, I don't think she liked me at all. Our last night together, she asked to open up the relationship. I think if she could have left me, she would have."

"Why did you upload her?" Aya's voice is gentle.

"I created NeuroNet so that you'd never have to say goodbye to the ones you love. What kind of asshole would I look like if I didn't upload my own wife?"

"You do not strike me as the kind of person who would care what others thought of her."

"When it could reflect badly on my work, I do," Teagan admits. "I also thought we could kill two birds with one stone if I went through with it . . . she had one of the potential suicide risk factors . . . Carter and Tito were surveilling her . . . I thought even if I didn't enjoy it, we might at least get a little closer to what went wrong with Dee Claybourne. Instead, I nearly got myself killed. What a colossal failure that was."

"Not necessarily." Aya turns a bright smile toward Teagan. "As long as you learn something, it is not a failure."

Teagan finds it difficult to laugh fully in the restraints, so she contents herself with a snort. "What did I learn?"

Aya's gaze is steady. "It sounds like you learned how to accept some hard truths and move on. That is progress." She extracts a box and places it by Teagan's side. "And I have a gift that should help ease your transition."

19

The sun rises over a wasted landscape, brown from neglect. Crows nibble at what seeds remain, obliterating the garden's potential.

Teagan turns away from the bay window and asks the household Eye, "What do you think? Should we pave over your garden and put up a parking lot?"

The Eye responds, "Nearest parking lot is 0.3 miles away. Traffic conditions are light. You should arrive there within two minutes. Would you like directions sent to your car?"

"No." Teagan shakes her head. "Sorry, I forgot." *Em is gone. For good.* It doesn't feel the way she imagined it would. There's no liberating feeling of freedom, only a dull heaviness.

Teagan's fingers tighten around the metal circlet she's holding—a Neural Nirvana headdress, an Aphrodite unit Aya gave her in the hospital. She has yet to put it on. "What's the point?" she'd asked Aya in the hospital. "I don't hate myself."

"Aphrodite has additional benefits," Aya had said. "You are grieving. You are a woman in transition. When was the last time you were single?"

"Thirty years?" She and Em started dating junior year of high school.

Aya smiled at that. "Do you even know who you are on your own?"

Teagan didn't like how she said that. "I've always been on my own."

Aya had audibly tsk-tsked. "You were children when you became a couple. You have never spent any alone time as an adult. It will be a hard transition. Aphrodite will help you understand who you are without Em and what you need to be happy alone."

"Is it therapy?" Teagan had laughed. "You make it sound like therapy."

"Aphrodite is better than therapy," Aya had said, pushing the headdress into Teagan's hands. "And you never have to tell anyone about it."

"I'm not ashamed of getting help," Teagan had lied.

"Good, then you will not mind using Aphrodite at least three times before coming back to work. To neutralize the trauma you have been through." When Teagan had opened her mouth to protest, Aya had added, "Carter and Tito have agreed, you must do this."

Teagan had taken the box from the hospital when they discharged her yesterday. She rambled around the home, avoiding it all day. But it's Sunday. If she wants to go back to work Monday, she needs to squeeze in three sessions. The headdress glows rose-gold. It matches all the appliances in the house. Teagan chuckles. "Em would have loved you." She centers it on her curls and scowls at the ridiculous-looking reflection of herself in the bay window. "Okay, Aphrodite: show me what you've got."

Her fingers depress a jewel-like button at the front-center of the circlet. Aphrodite hums to life.

She closes her eyes. *Surrender to the experience.*

After a few moments of surrender, she opens an eye. The window reflects what looks like a mad queen. *I look deranged standing up. Maybe it'll be easier to relax if I sit down?*

She sits in the breakfast nook, placing her hands on the table. That feels too formal. She moves them into her lap. There, they jerk around like hooked fish. She shakes her head. "I'm not good at relaxing. Is that something you can help with Aphrodite?"

In response, the headdress pulses. There's something in its reassuring thrum that sounds familiar. Teagan scans her body. Her typically tight shoulders aren't wound around her ears. *That's an improvement.* She waits to see what else might be different. *My mind is quieter.* That's big: thoughts tend to torment her, even when she's happy. *Maybe this is good for me, after all?*

The headdress pulses blithely on. That's when it hits her: what the sound is. It's the same sound a vibrator makes. *No wonder I feel better.*

Teagan can't help laughing at her own joke. She pictures a giant rose-gold dildo on her head, and when she doubles over, Aphrodite clatters to the table.

"Shoot." She picks it up. It hums happily in her hands. She thinks about sticking it in her lap, but there's no one here to appreciate her clowning. She turns it off. "Sorry. Don't want to break you on our maiden journey. I promise I'll try you again soon." *Ugh. I have to do this twice more today?*

She places it back in its box and pushes it out of sight. She's never been good with mindfulness activities. A lifetime ago, when Em and she were newlyweds, they tried going on yoga and meditation retreats together. It always felt good in the moment, but the tentatively won inner peace never lasted past Monday morning.

The iridescent icon on the box shimmers. Teagan traces the Neural Nirvana logo: a row of five spheres, then three, then a single sphere; all of them connected by arrows. At the launch party, she overheard a bearded gentleman explaining to his tipsy date that the icon symbolizes the tree of life. But it doesn't. It's a vertical diagram of an artificial neural network. The last sphere in the chain represents the human element. "The output."

The house is big and empty. Teagan can't think of anything she wants to do here. She calls Carter. His disembodied head floats in front of the bay window. She asks, "Are you busy?"

"No," he says, raising an eyebrow. "Rhys and I were just sitting down to breakfast."

"Do you mind if I join you?" She asks, even though she's not hungry.

To her relief, Carter does not turn her away. The whole car ride over, Teagan's mind is restless. She wants to go back to NeuroNet. *But is it too soon?* An old phrase pops into her head: 'not yet cold in her grave.' Em has a physical grave, where they deposited the body after she became Em-in-the-Eye. But they'd extracted everything that mattered when they uploaded her. She doesn't see the point in visiting it. *But would it help? Maybe I'm out of sorts because of grief? Maybe doing something like that—even if it's meaningless—would help?*

She is concerned about her lack of concern. She'd rather work than grieve. Grieving seems like a waste of time. *Maybe I spent too much time grieving what we lost when we were still together to feel anything now?* The first time Em left her, Teagan stayed in bed for a whole week. The second time, she only suffered for three days. By the third and fourth departures, Teagan felt ragged, but still managed to eat, shower, and get to work.

Perhaps I overestimated how much love I had left. The critical little voice inside her head adds, *Or underestimated my power of detachment.*

When Tito converted to Buddhism, he learned about the concept of three marriages and shared it with Teagan and Carter. "We are supposed to be married to our spouses, our work, and ourselves."

Carter and Teagan had laughed. She'd joked, "One out of three ain't bad, is it?"

Teagan watches house lights blur beneath her and braces for the decent into the familiar landing pad. *So many years ago, and work is still the only successful marriage any of us has been able to maintain.*

She presses her thumb into the biometric reader at the front door. The Eye announces her as the door slides away. As she steps into the foyer, Rhys comes skidding around the corner, curls bouncing. Teagan kneels to catch her goddaughter up in her arms. She attempts to lift her into an embrace but almost drops her when a spark passes between them.

Rhys's eyes widen. "What was that?" Her chubby hands grip her bare biceps.

"Not sure." Teagan rubs her own arms. "Static electricity? Must have been from you running and skidding all over the carpet in those stockinged feet!" She ruffles Rhys's hair. It feels thick and prickly with energy that nibbles at Teagan's fingers. "Maybe slow down next time?"

Carter emerges. There's a tumbler in each hand.

Teagan raises her eyebrows. "Double fisting it before noon?"

"I figured we could both use a stiff drink." He hands her one. "If it makes you happier, it's vodka. I could add some tomato juice and olives and turn it into a Bloody Mary."

"I'm not too hungry," Teagan admits. "Liquid diet will suit me fine."

Rhys screws up her face. "Don't get drunk! Daddy acts stupid when he's drunk."

Carter's jaw drops in mock hurt. "What?"

Teagan's brow furrows. "Your Daddy can be very silly. But stupid? He's never stupid."

Rhys stamps a little foot. "Mommy said drinking is bad for you."

"Hmm, well it's also fun, and can be an important way to blow off steam." Teagan exchanges a look with Carter. Rhys's value system would never evolve past a first-grader's black-and-white view of right and wrong. *What a drag.* "Everything in moderation, Rhys, including moderation. Follow that advice and you can't go wrong. I mean, you want your dad and me to have a little fun, right?"

Reluctantly, Rhys says, "Yes."

"Drinking can be bad if you do it too much, so I promise I'll keep your Dad in line." She almost says 'when you're old enough . . .' But Rhys will never be old enough to drink. *For that matter, she'll never grow up, fall in love, or have kids.* At the same time, it's not like Rhys is a real child. *I mean nothing bad would happen to her if we gave her a drink. Maybe we should?* But what would be the point? Would she enjoy it?

When Teagan was little, neighbors had trained their dog to drink beer. They thought it was funny, but it disturbed Teagan and her parents because the dog didn't know what was happening. Rhys wouldn't understand drinking either. That led Teagan to think of the Model Two sexbots . . . the ones designed to look like children. It spared real children from being sex trafficked, but did it affect the androids being used for that purpose?

Teagan doesn't know and she doesn't want to think of it anymore. *This needs to stop. These thoughts need to stop.* She wishes she hadn't left Aphrodite at home.

She notices Carter and Rhys are still looking at her. *Waiting for me to say something? Did I leave them hanging?* She smiles and says, "Best of all, drinking keeps you from thinking." She toasts Rhys and gestures to Carter. "And more than anything, that's what your Dad and I need."

"Why don't you take a nap while Aunt Teagan and I catch up?" Carter says. Rhys groans, but obediently makes her way up the winding staircase. He winks at Teagan. "I'll be right back."

Teagan watches them climb the stairs: a guardian and his child. *Loved ones aren't the only ones frozen. The guardians are as caught up as the bots are in familiar patterns. Does ministering to loved ones stunt their growth, too?* The question amuses her. "Since when do you care about growth? You've eaten the same thing for breakfast for the past twenty years."

Laughing, Teagan makes her way into the sitting room. Melody's touch remains strong here: lavender sofas, chairs, and a loveseat, impressionistic swirls of art grace the walls, and the lamps glow softly. It is a soothing room. Teagan is reminded of the Aphrodite chamber at the Neural Nirvana launch, minus the socialites and hangers-on. She hears a step on the tiles behind her and turns. "That didn't take long."

Carter shrugs and heads to the bar cart to refresh his drink. "She doesn't mind if I skip story time now and then."

"Would she ever really mind?"

Carter fixes her with a quizzical look. "You're in an odd mood. What's up?"

Teagan settles into the loveseat. "My mind is racing. I thought coming over might distract me from some of my thoughts."

He frowns. "Bad ones?"

Teagan shakes her head. "I wouldn't say bad or good. They're . . . constant. Like I can't turn my mind off. It's a lot of noise."

Carter nods. "Have you tried Aya's headdress?"

"Yes."

"Did it work?"

Teagan's mouth twists as she considers his question. "I'm not sure what it's supposed to do or how I'm supposed to feel. And how often? For how long? Aya was incredibly cryptic."

"That's Aya," Carter says. He throws a celery stick in his drink. "There, now I've a balanced breakfast."

Teagan smiles, but she doesn't like how casually he said Aya's name. Normally it comes out like he's trying not to swallow something sour. "What's up?"

He looks up, surprised. "What do you mean?"

"You almost sounded friendly when you mentioned Aya. Did you kiss and make up while I was away?"

"Hardly," he scoffs.

"What then? You're not cursing her name. Something big must have happened."

He rises and reaches for her glass. "Let me freshen that up."

Teagan resists. "Carter Bryson Smith! Don't you dare change the subject on me."

He takes her glass anyway. "I'm not changing the subject. It's not a big mystery. Aya's saving our ass with her investment. It's taken a huge weight off me. And she's keeping the other investors calm. What? Did you expect me to hold a grudge forever?"

"And they say old dogs can't learn new tricks."

He straightens up and throws a haughty look over his shoulder. "You know how I feel about *them*."

It's so comfortable being back in rhythm with her best friend. "You're right. To hell with *them*." He hands her a full glass, ice cubes tinkling softly.

This is nice. It's homey, being with Carter like this. Life without Em is good. *Easier.*

KRISTI CASEY

Teagan swirls the vodka around before saying what she came here to ask. "Hey . . . I know they would say it's too early, but I really want to come back to work. Would it be okay if I came back tomorrow?"

"Please do." Carter smiles. "Please come back tomorrow. To hell with *them*."

20

The morning skies are dark, but Teagan's heart is light. *Work will be good for me.*

Her mouth twists. When Em was alive, Teagan worked to escape. *What am I escaping now?*

Maybe myself?

She had spent all day with Carter and Rhys. By the time she came home, it was time for bed.

Aya might be right. I need to learn how to be comfortable living on my own.

She removes the headdress from its shimmery box.

Maybe if I do an extra-long session, it can count as sessions two and three, combined?

It might be a trick of the light, but Aphrodite appears to shimmer in her hands. She rotates it slowly before putting it on. When it hums to life, Teagan swears she can see a tiny light glimmering around the corners of her vision. She narrows her eyes to try and see better. There's a sweet spot with them half-shut that gives the illusion of fairy lights twinkling. Her breath slows. *This is nice.* She couldn't sleep at all last night. Just stayed up, staring at the ceiling until it was time to get up and shower.

Deep waves of calm ripple through Teagan, emanating from the crown of her head, through her torso, and down into the breakfast nook seat. *This is better than sleeping.*

Teagan's eyes are drawn to a slideshow endlessly scrolling on the opposite wall. *Our greatest hits,* Teagan thinks, but the sting has gone out of that phrase. She feels so peaceful, enveloped by Aphrodite's blissful thrum, that she watches the pictures spool without judgment. *We were both so young. And happy.* She watches the pictures of her and Em goofing around at school, kissing in front of a sunset, cheering at one of Rhys's soccer games, and on the town with Melody and Carter, in matching tuxedos for a fancy charity ball.

Teagan's hand drifts to her face. There's a smile there. It matches the one she sees on screen. *We were so happy.*

Teagan scans her body. The nanobots must have done their job because she doesn't even feel achy. She turns Aphrodite off and places it gently in its box. She catches her reflection in the glass and it startles her. *I look ten years younger. Nice work Aphrodite.*

The sky opens, sending sheets of rain down. The parched earth of the garden becomes muddy. Teagan watches the rain pound the seed pods of wasted plants and wonders what will happen if she leaves it to itself. *Will it grow and heal?*

It's getting late. She doesn't want to be late on her first day back. She backs her car out of the garage and into the skies. The rain pelts the windshield making it difficult to see anything. The car's Eye informs her it's the remnants of a hurricane that made landfall in Florida just before dawn. She remembers when hurricane season was a season. Now they hit whenever. It's a pity. She used to like some of the cities there when she was a girl on family trips south. So many are now underwater.

There are far more dangerous weather days than there used to be. *Maybe it's time for me to appreciate the beautiful ones more instead of fearing them.*

The Executive Suite Eye meets her at the landing pad with a plastic disc meant to shield her from the rain. Teagan walks its artificially dry path. Carter waits behind the glass door for her. He reminds her of a puppy, so eager for her return.

The door slides away. She grins. "What? No flowers?"

"Do you need them to know how happy I am to have you back?"

She hugs him. "I'm glad to be back, too. Where should I start?"

Carter takes her purse and sets it down on the marshmallow pouf. "Let's go to the lab. I want you to meet someone. Tito's got a new team member."

"Oh?" Tito's notoriously selective. He hasn't added anyone to his team in five years. "It must be someone special."

"Yes," Carter says. The door to the hallway opens for them. He calls the elevator. "She's a recent grad, but head and shoulders above most of the engineers you probably know. A real prodigy."

"Where'd she come from?" It's unusual for Carter to gush about anyone. Teagan can tell he's genuinely excited. "What's her specialty?"

"Tech. And hybrid neural networks."

"Huh." The elevator gently lurches under their weight. Designing hybrid neural networks is Teagan's specialty. And Tech is just down the street. It's been twenty-something years since they graduated. It's still one of the best engineering schools. But something feels off. *Why is he so excited?*

The elevator doors open. She follows Carter into the hallway. "This is my first day back. Are you trying to replace me already?"

Carter grins over his shoulder and thumbs the biometric pad outside the lab. Unlike the antiseptic lighting in the upload bays, the lighting here is amber and pink, carefully calibrated with the screens to reduce eye strain and promote a feeling of relaxation—one of Aya's last contributions to NeuroNet before her departure. Many of the technicians never leave. Why would they? In addition to a cafeteria and game area, there are cots and showers, a gymnasium, and a quiet room. It's like a dorm for overgrown misfit kids. Teagan wonders if the people on Tito's team even have homes. She doubts Tito does. He keeps a rack with clothes in his office. He's never invited her or Carter over.

Tito is in his office, but he's not alone. A woman Teagan doesn't recognize sits by his side, discussing something on the screen between them.

"She's only been here a couple of days?" Carter nods. Teagan frowns. Tito and the women are intimately comfortable with each other. She whispers to Carter, "Is he fucking her?"

Carter barks a laugh. "God, I hope not!"

Tito and the woman look up. Teagan raises a hand in greeting. "Hi!"

The woman rises and Teagan is struck by a sense of *déja-vu*. "Hi, I'm Allie." She extends a hand in greeting.

"Teagan." Teagan takes her slender, tan hand and shakes it. She knows they've never met, but there's something about Allie's long brown hair and golden eyes that Teagan recognizes. "Sorry. I don't mean to stare, but—God—you look so much like . . ." She can't say the name. She looks at Carter. *Does he see it, too?*

He must. He nods and says, "Melody. I know. She looks like Melody."

"They could be twins." Teagan studies him, but his face remains impassive. *Maybe he finds the resemblance comforting?* Teagan resolves that if Carter's not freaked out by someone looking like his dead wife, she won't be either.

Tito laughs. "Isn't it incredible? She looks like Melody, but she thinks just like you!"

"Me?" Teagan smiles at Allie. "I'm sorry. If that's true, you must have a lot of trouble at parties."

Allie replies dryly, "Yeah, you have to keep me from swinging on the chandeliers."

The woman's wit takes her by surprise. *We have the same sense of humor.* The thought stirs something like revulsion. Teagan chides herself: *You don't even know her. Why don't you like her?* She takes a deep breath and sits. *Best to refocus on work. Anything else is a waste of time.* "What are you working on?"

Tito pivots the screens so Carter and Teagan can see. "Allie's helping me take another look at the cognitive dashboards. She's found something interesting."

Allie nods. "As you know, your original assumption was that an aberrant action—like Dee's suicide—would be preceded by some kind of cognitive spike."

"Right, but that's not what we found," Teagan said. "There aren't any patterns."

Allie's face lights up. "Wrong!" She speaks with such enthusiasm that Teagan wants to punch her in the neck. Allie pinches and zooms three dashboards, carefully overlaying them and highlighting, what to Teagan's dismay, forms a distinct pattern.

Teagan's heart sinks. She can tell from the expression on the boys' faces that they've already seen this Eureka moment. It's being recreated for her benefit. *Why are you upset rather than excited? Are you the only one allowed to have epiphanies?* She needs to be better than petty. She takes a deep breath and asks, "What am I looking at?"

Allie's so excited that her words tumble out over one another. Teagan's taken aback until she remembers that she does the same thing. *It's a cliché to tear down other women, I should be supportive. After all, we've needed a breakthrough. If it comes from her, you should be thankful. See if you can focus on finding things you like about her rather than picking her apart.* But by the time Teagan finishes her inner monologue, she realizes she's missed Allie's entire explanation. "I'm sorry, can you repeat that?"

Allie patiently shares, "There is a pattern. But it's not a giant spike. It's a circular thought pattern. It's like the bot's cognitive process got caught in a loop." She points to one of the dashboards. "This is one circuit pass. It's hard to see when you're looking at the big picture because it's not true dissonance, per se. No spikes. But the consistency of the thoughts must create their own kind of dissonance." Allie's fingers overlay the three data snapshots, lining them up along the highlighted points. Now what's wrong about it jumps off the screen, clear as day to Teagan.

How did I miss that before? She mulls it over. "They're stuck in a loop . . . You think they commit suicide to break the cycle?"

"To get unstuck?" Allie nods. "Yes, I do."

Teagan frowns. "But technically, all the uploads are stuck, aren't they? I mean, with the AI gated, they can't evolve. They're stuck with the same habits they had in life, repeating the same routine responses."

"True," Allie says. "But so do living people. And most of them have no problem living like that. I mean, don't you know people who eat the same breakfast every day?"

Teagan feels Carter and Tito looking at her. "Of course." She makes a mental note to try something other than avocado toast tomorrow.

Allie continues. "That doesn't mean they're depressed, or unhappy with life."

"True." Teagan relaxes.

"But it's not for everyone. I mean, some people don't like repetition or habits, or patterns. Some people go out of their way to avoid predictable behavior."

Teagan and Em had fought about that once. Em had insisted that she never did the same thing twice. Her resistance to admit to any habits had driven Teagan mad. She failed to get Em to admit to even brushing her teeth the same way twice. Teagan herself did many things habitually. It was a comfort. But Allie brings up a good question: *What if people who avoid habitual behavior have a harder time adjusting to uploaded life?*

Teagan's brows furrow. "I agree with your statement. Let's assume that it applies to both Dee Claybourne's suicide and Em's . . ." She struggles to produce the right word. "Rebellion." *Not quite right, but it will have to do.* "But Dee Claybourne was uploaded a dozen years ago. Em only lasted a couple of days. How do you explain the difference between them? Or the variables between the other suicides we've seen? Is there a tipping point? An outside trigger?"

Allie frowns. "I'm not sure yet."

Teagan nods. This girl isn't going to replace her anytime soon. *But I should get to know her. She's bright and can help.* "What are you doing for lunch?"

"Um . . ." Allie looks at Tito and Carter.

Tito pushes aside the screens to get a direct view of her. "We were going to order delivery. Pizza or something."

"Nonsense," Teagan says. "Why don't I take Allie out? I'd like to pursue this line of thought further."

Carter frowns. "Where were you thinking of going?"

"We'll stay in the neighborhood, so we can be back in a jiffy if you need us," Teagan assures him. His face relaxes. Teagan asks, "Does Stinky's still serve food?"

Carter's nose wrinkles. "You want to go to Stinky's Pub? They were bad twenty years ago."

Teagan shrugs. "I'm feeling nostalgic."

"They still serve food," Tito says. "I go there often."

Teagan smiles. "I'm glad at least one of us still does."

Tito laughs. "How could I abandon Stinky's? It's where NeuroNet was born!"

Stinky's Pub had been their default hangout in college. Where she, Tito, Aya, and Carter had cemented their partnership. The napkin sketch that became NeuroNet bears a Stinky's logo on it.

"I wish I hadn't, but Em hated it." Teagan admits.

"So did Melody," Carter adds. He still doesn't look comfortable.

Teagan tells him, "It doesn't matter if the food is good or not—apologies Allie—I mainly want to go over Allie's discovery and talk through some of the implications."

Carter and Tito exchange a look. Tito replies first. "That's a great idea." Before Carter can say anything, Tito repeats, "It's a great idea. Do you want Carter and I to come with you?"

"No." She wants to understand who this Allie is without their interference. And—if she really is brilliant—they'll discover more by themselves without the boys jumping all over their ideas. She turns to the eerily beautiful new lab assistant. "Is that okay with you?"

Allie nods and meets her gaze with one that doesn't contain any fear or uncertainty. "Of course."

21

As they wait for the elevator, Allie frowns. "Are you sure you don't want to take the car?"

Teagan hits the lobby button. "It's only a few blocks. We'll be fine."

Allie joins her and the doors close. "I've always wondered if it's really as dangerous as they say it is on the surface streets."

Teagan smirks. "Well, you know what *they* say . . ."

"Who are *they* and why should *we* care?" Allie looks proud of herself.

Teagan forces herself to smile but inside, she fumes. *I can't believe Carter's already shared that joke with her.* "We'll slip out the back, by the loading ramp. You don't want to have to wade through the protesters out front."

"Are they always there?"

Teagan rolls her eyes. "Nonstop. It's been worse since the Claybourne incident."

They slip out, round the corner, and cross the street. Allie keeps pace with her easily. That's good. Having to slow down for slow walkers is one of Teagan's pet peeves.

The quickest way is through an underpass. Teagan hesitates but decides to forge ahead. It seems stupid to walk around the block when she can see the sign for the bar twinkling in the sunlight, just past the low-slung bridge.

They walk awhile in silence. Then, Allie says, "I haven't been to Stinky's for ages."

Teagan stops in the middle of the road. "Why would you ever go?"

Allie blushes. The words tumble out, "Oh, I used to go all the time when I was at Tech. They had the best wings."

A car horn reminds Teagan to get out of the way. She jumps the curb onto the sidewalk. "I'd ask about which professors you had, but I'm sure anyone who taught me retired before you enrolled. You look like a baby."

Allie laughs. "I'm not that young."

Teagan gives her the side-eye. There's something familiar about that laugh. Something Teagan doesn't like, although she can't pin it down. *Is she flirting with me?* That would be so inappropriate. *But maybe that's her strategy? Get us under her spell . . . Tito and Carter are clearly smitten.* It's a gross thought. *And maybe it says more about me than her. Something about her really irritates me.*

The exterior of the pub has resisted all attempts to upgrade it. Flakes of varnish curl around Teagan's hand as she opens the door and waves Allie through. The sun plays over the young woman's face and Teagan thinks again of Melody. *God, I miss her.* Melody pops to mind every time Teagan sees Rhys. The child resembles her so strongly. *But when was the last time I really thought about what I loved about her?* The Melody of her memories is always dead or dying. *But she was smart and funny. She made an amazing banana bread. She never forgot a birthday. She let me vent without judgement. And she kept Carter in line.*

Carter.

Teagan can tell he's in trouble. Sometimes she can smell the tang of alcohol on him at work. *Was he always destined to become an alcoholic like his dad? Or is it only because he lost her, too?*

"Are you coming?"

Teagan releases the door and follows Allie into Stinky's. "Sorry. You look so much like someone I used to know. I'm afraid it sent me down a little rabbit hole."

Her eyebrows raise. "Carter's wife?"

"Yeah." It's so striking a resemblance, Teagan knows she shouldn't be surprised, but she is. "Did he mention it?"

Allie nods and takes a seat by the bar. "He did. It's awful what happened."

"How did you—?"

"It was all over the news when I was a kid," Allie says. "I grew up around the corner. Stupid accident."

"It could have been avoided if the driver had his automatic settings on," Teagan says. "But I guess he didn't trust the tech? It was still new tech at the time."

"It's too bad." Allie pats at the bar.

Teagan imagines Allie's looking for the least sticky place to rest her arms. That's what Teagan is doing. "It is. So many lives are saved when we don't rely on human impulses."

The edge of the bar glows. The air in front of them flickers as a menu appears. Allie chuckles. "This is new."

"Fancy." Teagan scrolls the items and selects a basket of lemon-pepper wings.

"Those are my favorite, too." Allie's eyes twinkle. "Should we get pints of beer to wash them down?"

Teagan's mouth is dry. An IPA would be nice. But she doesn't want to invite any scrutiny. "I don't think that's appropriate."

Allie nods. "Of course."

Teagan studies the young woman's profile. *She may be smart, but she lacks good judgement. Why would she think I'd want to do that?* She shoves away the acknowledgement that beer is exactly what she wants. Especially with lemon-pepper wings. *Maybe that's what she did with Carter and Tito and thinks I'd be open to that, too?*

Once again Allie's familiarity with the boys irks Teagan. *Well, she guessed wrong.*

An Eye deposits waters and napkin-wrapped silverware. Allie wets a napkin and wipes her portion of the bar. The napkin comes apart in her hands. "They should have named this bar 'Sticky's.'"

Teagan laughs. Fragments of napkin stay attached to the bar as Teagan unwraps the fork and knife. "Not much has changed."

Allie tilts her head. "It's crazy to think that this is where NeuroNet was born."

Teagan taps the bar. "I sketched out the framework for NeuroNet with cocktail peanuts right here."

"Quite an achievement," Allie says. "You should be proud of yourself."

"Hmm." Teagan's pride is mixed with something else. *What? Nostalgia for who Carter and I were? For enthusiasm I no longer feel?* This is another rabbit hole, best to avoid. "It's a trap to feel too much pride in past achievements. I'd rather focus on what's in front of me. Keep learning and growing."

Allie glows with youth and good health. It reminds Teagan of what she will never have again. "Tell me: how did you discover the dissonance was disguised in a loop?"

"Tito shared what you'd already examined. It was thorough. But . . ." Allie shrugs. "I just looked at the data differently. And when I did, it was obvious what was happening."

Teagan wishes she had the breakthrough, not Allie. "Can we write an algorithm to detect the loop in others?"

"Not yet." The corner of Allie's mouth twitches. "With a dataset of three? We don't have enough information."

"We can't wait for more bots to malfunction."

Allie looks down. "I don't know if they are malfunctioning."

Teagan leans in. "What do you mean?"

Allie frowns. "Tito ever share his funny sayings with you?"

Teagan's hand reaches for the piece of jade he gave her on impulse. She releases it almost as quickly, feeling ridiculously superstitious. "Tito says a lot of things."

"I mean what his Grams always says."

There is only one thing Teagan remembers Tito ever saying about his grandfather. "Don't die like an octopus, cark it like a hammerhead shark?"

"Yes!" One of Allie's eyes is caught in a sunbeam. It glitters fervently.

Never mind.

"He says it, but I don't really know what that has to do with . . ."

"The loved ones?" Allie's smile is tight and smug. "Most of our loved ones are octopi. When you catch an octopus, it doesn't fight. It gives up. It's easy to subdue and kill. But a hammerhead shark . . . Even after you kill it, it continues to fight."

Teagan considers that. "Are you saying that some people's consciousnesses resist being uploaded?"

"I don't know if it's that clear-cut." Allie chews on her bottom lip. "But I do think there's something to that idea. What if some people don't mind being stuck? When they transition to a bodiless state and find themselves in a mental state that doesn't evolve, maybe it's similar enough to how they lived their lives that they don't even notice they're in a holding pattern."

Teagan laughs. "By that assessment, I'd make a good upload candidate."

"There's nothing about your life you'd want to change?" Allie's eyes look at Teagan intently.

Teagan scratches at a piece of stuck napkin. "Actually . . . I've been thinking about adjustments I need to make."

Allie leans in. "Really? Like what?"

Teagan laughs. "It's insignificant, really. Not even worth mentioning. But my wife used to tease me about eating the same thing for breakfast. I was thinking I'd try something different tomorrow."

Allie's eyes widen. "Wow. That's a big step."

"Not really." Teagan isn't sure if Allie is teasing her or not. "I mean, it's not like I'm intending to climb Mt. Everest or anything. It's just breakfast."

Allie's mouth opens as if she has something to add but closes it quickly. She doesn't speak again until they finish consuming their lunch. Then, she asks, "Should we get a cab?"

Teagan shrugs. "You're welcome to, but I'm going to walk. It's quicker." She heads to the door and Allie follows.

A sandy-haired man doesn't wait for Teagan to pass by at the exit. He squeezes into the small arrival lobby, pressing uncomfortably close to her. Before she can reach the street, two more men—the sandy-haired one's friends, she assumes—push past rudely.

They stop to leer at Allie. "Hey babe."

Teagan grabs Allie's arm and grumbles, "Fucking jerks." She pushes past the gauntlet of men and pulls them outside. It's so bright. She releases Allie's arm so she can shield her eyes. "Sorry. Did I grab you too roughly?"

Allie shakes her head. Her brow furrows in concern. "Are you sure you don't want to summon a ride?"

"It'd be a waste of time and money. It's only a 10-minute walk." She presses on and soon hears Allie walking along behind her.

A voice rings out. "Hey!"

Teagan sighs. She knows without turning who it must be. She's not surprised to see the sandy-haired man and his two friends scowling on the sidewalk. *Shit.*

"I think you owe us an apology," the man says.

Teagan turns around and keeps walking.

"Hey," the man shouts again. "I think you owe me an apology."

"Fuck you," Teagan calls over her shoulder. *Entitled pricks.*

He roars back, "Fuck you, you stuck-up bitch!"

"Teagan!" Allie hisses.

"What?" Teagan darts a quick look at Allie. "If anything, he should apologize to us for being rude and gross." But she can hear the men behind them. "We need to pick up the pace." She surveils the path ahead. She asks Allie, "Can you run in those heels?" Allie nods. Teagan mutters low. "I don't want them to catch us by the overpass. It's too dark and deserted. But I think we'll be safe if we can get to the other side. They won't do anything in front of NeuroNet. Too many people there who could see them. Ready to run?"

Allie nods.

"Okay, go!"

Teagan can't remember the last time she ran. *Maybe with Carter? When we were kids?* It's an awkward business. Not something she—or Allie, apparently—is good at.

A memory she's buried resurfaces. *Oh no.* She runs faster. *Maybe this time, they won't catch me.* She hasn't thought about that attack in years. She froze then. Gave in. *I won't let that happen again.*

The hulking overpass blocks out the sun. A bright rectangle of light marks their goal. *Safety. We can make it.*

"Oh no, you don't." A hand tightens on her upper arm. Teagan's body jerks in a wide arch. The hand yanks her back until she's nose to nose with the sandy-haired man.

Not again. Never again, she thinks. She shoves his chest, ready to fight him off.

But he grips her other arm and pulls her close. "C'mon, now," he says, pushing her against a low retaining wall. "I just want to talk."

The concrete bites her lower back. "This is not how you talk to people." She tries to push him away.

"Don't talk back to me, you bitch." He slaps her.

It's shocking, the violence of it. Last time she was in a position like this, she didn't fight. She was too scared. *What if he gets mad at me?* She was afraid fighting would make it worse. Giving up didn't make what followed less painful.

I won't make that mistake again. The light under the overpass is dingy. It's hard to see anything. *But maybe there's something here I can use as a weapon?* She feels around the edge of the wall as he presses closer. *There's got to be something I can use to defend myself.*

Allie must be on her left with the other two men. There's the sound of shuffling feet and sudden stops from just beyond Teagan's vision. *They must be toying with her, enjoying her fright.*

"You need to let us go," Teagan tells the sandy-haired man.

"Or what?" He smirks. "What do you think you are going to do?"

Something hard and cold within Teagan rises to the surface. It's not fear. It's a decision. *I need to stop him from hurting me. And from hurting anyone else. Ever.* Her chin rises stubbornly. She says with calm resolve, "I will give you until the count of ten to turn and walk away."

He laughs. "What if I don't want to?"

"I will give you until the count of ten." *I am not going to be the soft target he wants. I'll fight him. I'll fight all of them.* "Tell your friends and go."

Or what? Kill him? She's not sure. But she has the right to defend herself. *Could I kill him?* The cold, hard center of her feels capable of it, even if his physical advantage makes that unlikely.

He needs to leave me alone, or I might kill him. The thought feels true. *And I might enjoy it.* She might. Afraid of how much she might enjoy hurting this man who wants to hurt her, she warns him again. "Seriously, you and your friends need to leave. I'll give you till the count of ten."

He laughs. She begins a slow count: "One."

The man takes a step back. "What the hell?" He looks at his friends. They stop pushing Allie around.

"Two." Teagan hopes Allie's smart enough to run for safety if she gets the chance. She doesn't want to get distracted trying to protect them both. "Three."

How can I protect myself? Her mind spools through a catalog of workshop maneuvers she learned in a self-defense class.

"Four." *Honestly, would it be that bad if he died? He wouldn't be able to hurt anyone else.*

"Five." Now her mind is exploring ways she might be able to kill him. *I think the heel of my hand, if it hit his nose at just the right angle, might send the cartilage to his brain. That would kill him, right? Or could I snap his neck?*

"Six." Her hand continues to search the ledge for some kind of weapon. She's glad it's so dark. He hasn't noticed her furtive movements.

"Seven." Something rough is underneath her right hand. *What is this?* It's sharp. That's promising.

The men are still, but they're starting to smirk. Teagan can feel their confusion turning ugly again.

"Eight." Whatever it is she grips cuts deep. Her hand is slick.

"Nine." She pulls her arm in close, ready to attack.

"Ten."

The sandy-haired man sneers. He looks at his friends and they laugh. His smile drops. "You stupid bitch." He lunges at Teagan.

Everything happens in slow motion. The sharp object in her hand connects with his skull. She feels it hit something soft. She pushes until it hits the bone and scrapes the edge of his eye socket. She feels something pop out.

His screams puncture the dim, confusing space between them. He backs away, hands at his face. It takes Teagan a moment to process what she's seeing. It's a bloody socket where his right eye should be. The eye dangling, attached by an impossibly slender nerve. Liquid spews from the socket, where a wedge of glass sits. His left hand clutches at it, trying to pull it free. But the pain of extraction must be greater than the desire to be free of it. Or perhaps the glass and his hand are too slick with blood to get a grip.

Is that a beer bottle shard? It's a ridiculous sight, like one of those fake victims in a haunted house. The eye bouncing against his cheekbone doesn't look real.

No one moves. Everyone is frozen, watching the horrible jig of the one-eyed sandy-haired man.

Teagan's spell breaks first. She grabs Allie's arm and pulls her into a run. The men shout, but no footsteps ring out. Teagan and Allie leave them to tend to their wounded leader.

The women emerge from the overpass and Teagan doesn't check if the light is green. As they run across the four lanes toward the traffic island, surface-bound cars screech to a halt, stopped by their automatic safety systems. Teagan leans against the light pole and pushes the walk button to take them to the other side. A flood of relief washes over her. She laughs.

Allie's eyes widen. "Why are you laughing? A man was seriously injured."

Teagan straightens up. All mirth drains away. "Would you rather he injured us?"

"No, but—"

"That's what he meant to do. What they all meant to do."

Allie's lips thin to a tight line of disapproval. "You attacked him."

What is she angry about? "Would you rather I let him rape us?"

"Of course not!"

Teagan's mind races with all the reasons why Allie should be expressing gratitude. "Then I think you should thank me for helping us get out of that situation. You certainly didn't help."

"No." Her eyes darken. "No, I froze. I always freeze."

Teagan's chin juts out stubbornly. "Well, I didn't feel like being a victim today. And I bet he'll think twice about doing this to anyone ever again. We have a right to defend ourselves."

Allie shakes her head. "I can't believe you'd hurt someone."

The walk sign lights up. "C'mon." Teagan doesn't wait to see if Allie is behind her. She jogs across the street. It isn't until she steps onto the sidewalk in front of NeuroNet that she realizes her mistake. In her haste to get inside, she forgot to curve around to the loading dock. Now she's on the edge of a sea of protesters.

Allie grabs her elbow. It's almost painful, the jolt of it. Teagan looks over her shoulder. Allie's eyes are wide. "We shouldn't run through that gauntlet." Her eyes drop. "You're hurt."

Teagan follows Allie's gaze and is shocked to see her right hand is gushing blood. She looks behind her and, sure enough, there's the faintest trace of a bloody trail stretching back toward the overpass. She rips a strip off her shirt to wind around it. "It must be shock. I don't feel a thing."

Allie's brows knit. "We should head to the side door."

Teagan sighs. "Fuck that. I'm tired of running. Maybe we can sneak by them without causing a scene."

The protesters appear to be at rest. Most of them are milling around, signs loosely held at chest-level or resting on their shoes. Teagan lowers her head, hoping to squeak by unnoticed. Her eyes scan the visible signs:

FREE THE UPLOADS
WHAT ABOUT THE OTHER 99%?
UPLOAD RIGHTS ARE HUMAN RIGHTS!

Some are religious in tone:

GOD HATES NEURONET
EXODUS 20:3
CARTER-MCKENNA-NGATA: UNHOLY TRINITY

Teagan imagines she, Tito, and Carter dressed up as devils, painted red and holding pitchforks. She giggles.

Allie pokes her. "What are you laughing at, Teagan?"

"Teagan?" A tall, gaunt man steps in front of Teagan. She instinctively looks up. "Hey, I know you."

Teagan pushes past him.

He yells to the crowd: "That's Dr. McKenna!"

The group of aimless protesters unite in sudden, violent activity. Teagan feels the knot of them tighten around her. The anger in their eyes concerns her more than the sandy-haired man's. She knew what he wanted. There's no telling what these people want as an endgame. "Allie, we're going to have to fight our way through."

"No!" Allie looks at Teagan as if she is insane. "We can't do that!"

"Then you can stay here and try to reason with them." Teagan says, lowering her shoulder and bulldozing a woman out of her way. A hand slips into her mouth. Teagan bites it. Someone tugs at her hair, rips her sleeve.

There's a gap in the crowd. A buzzing sound from overhead. *What's happening?* She looks up. Drones circle overhead, threatening the release of gas.

It's their security system for crowd control. *Thank God. Tito must be watching.* "Allie!" Teagan cries. "Allie! Cover your mouth and nose. Now!"

The drones drop tear gas canisters. The smoke infiltrates the fleshy mob. The people holding Teagan cough and fall away. Teagan grabs Allie's sleeve. Clutching the cloth of their shirts to their faces, they reach the glass doors. The security Eyes let them in and seal out the mob.

Allie's face is covered in scratches. Teagan tenderly examines it. "We need medical attention."

Allie shakes her head. "It's not bad. Tito can patch us up in the lab."

Teagan wants to argue, but she senses someone approaching. She swings around to confront them, then relaxes once she recognizes the journalist. "Roz?" She's never been in the same room with the *Humanity Now* reporter. *She looks taller than on the vids.*

"Oh my God," Roz says. "You've been attacked?"

Teagan can't share any of this until she's talked with Ascha and the boys. "What are you doing here?"

Allie tugs at her. "The elevator . . ."

Roz says, "I've been trying to reach you."

"I haven't had time to even check my messages," Teagan says. "And we ran into a bit of trouble. What's up?"

Roz looks uncertain about talking in front of Allie. "Can we go somewhere and talk in private?"

Allie pulls Teagan toward the elevator.

Teagan says, "This isn't a good time. Can I call you later?"

"I'm afraid it's time-sensitive," Roz says. "There's a story I'm going to break tonight. I want to give you a chance to comment."

"I'm sorry, Roz," Allie says, punching the button for the lab. "We need to get back to work."

Teagan shoots Allie a look. *Who the hell does she think she is?* She looks apologetically at Roz. Before the elevator doors close on them, Teagan squeaks out, "Contact Ascha. She'll take care of you."

22

Tito's horrified face tells Teagan everything she needs to know about what she and Allie must look like. She attempts to deflect his horror with humor. "Spoiler alert. Walking to Stinky's wasn't smart."

He doesn't laugh the way she hopes. "You've got a car. Why the hell did you walk? Do you have a death wish?"

"I didn't think it would be as bad as everyone says." Teagan attempts another joke. "Besides, you know how tough it is to find parking in Midtown. It's much faster to walk."

Tito frowns. "Not funny. You're not being funny." He fetches the lab's first aid kit.

"Not even a little bit?" Teagan leans in, but Tito doesn't crack a smile. *He must be really pissed.*

"Get up on the table and give me your hand."

Teagan obliges and places her hand in his. The strip of shirt she's wound around her is crimson and wet with blood.

"Jesus." He searches her eyes. "The protesters did this?"

"No. This was the cost of defending our honor." She smiles at Allie, but the woman's stone-faced demeanor rebuffs her. Teagan jerks a thumb toward her. "She would have rather been raped."

"Teagan!" Allie sounds scandalized. "That's not funny."

Tito's brow crinkles, releasing his glasses. "Wait." They bounce down onto the bridge of his nose. "What are you talking about?"

Allie sighs. "Some guys followed us out of the bar."

Teagan rolls her eyes. "You make it sound so innocent." She tells Tito, "They chased us, caught us under the underpass, and probably would have raped and murdered us if I hadn't fought back."

Tito frowns. He looks to Allie and back to Teagan. "You fought back? How?"

Tired of waiting for him to address her bleeding hand, she unwinds the cloth herself. "I grabbed a piece of glass and shoved it into the lead guy's face."

"Oh my God!" Tito grabs his chest.

It reminds Teagan of a meme from her childhood. "Uh-oh, Elizabeth," she says. "It's the big one!"

Allie laughs, then catches herself and rearranges her face to look disapproving. Teagan smirks. *Got you.*

"Will you stop mucking about?" Tito is dabbing at her cut with gauze. "You could have been killed. Or worse. You're acting like a Muppet."

Teagan knows from experience that when Tito uses Kiwi slang, he's not happy. "I guess. Maybe I'm in shock. I can't even feel my hand."

Allie tries to hand Tito a small green vial. He waves her away. "I need the peroxide." He swabs Teagan's wound with it and continues his lecture. "I can't believe how irresponsible you were. Taking two of our most valuable assets and putting them in danger."

Teagan pulls her hand back. "Excuse me?" She gestures to Allie. "*Two* of our most valuable assets? First, I'm not an object, I'm a *person.* Second—and no offense to Allie—but how the hell is she important, at all?"

"No offense taken," Allie says.

Teagan looks at her hand. "I think something's wrong with your peroxide. It's not fizzing."

"It's fine," Tito says. He bandages her hand with clean gauze.

Teagan watches the top of his head as he works. There's a little patch of skin visible under thinning hair. *Jeez, Tito's going bald? We're all getting so old.* She examines his handiwork. "I'm probably going to need stitches. Maybe I should go to the hospital?"

Tito shakes his head. "I don't think so. It didn't look like there was any infection or any debris caught in the wound. I think it will heal on its own."

Teagan shrugs. "Whatever you say, you're the doctor."

"Technically, the biologist," Allie retorts.

Teagan frowns at her. "If you want to be really technical: neurobiological engineer." Teagan knows she snapped back a little too sharply, but she couldn't help it. *It's too bad I don't like her. I want to. But she keeps rubbing me the wrong way.*

Teagan debates saying something to Carter and Tito. But what would she say? '*That new hire you love is annoying?*' Maybe she is overreacting. *This is my first day back. Carter and Tito must like Allie for a reason. If I raise a stink, they'll chalk it up to jealousy rather than hear me out.*

Teagan lingers over that thought. *Am I jealous?*

Tito's hand pats her arm. She looks up, questioning.

"Your injury is going to cock up the scan pads. I need to get new scans of your left hand to give you security clearance on the biometric pads."

Teagan gives him her left hand. She can feel Allie's eyes burning a hole in her head. "What?"

Allie frowns. "You weren't scared?"

Teagan scoffs.

Tito admonishes her, "Hey, be still. I'm not done. I need five seconds for each imprint."

Teagan sticks her tongue out. Allie clears her throat. Teagan glances her way. "Scared of what? The protesters?"

"No . . ." Allie looks at Tito as if she's wishing he weren't in the room.

"We don't have to talk about this now if you don't want to," Teagan offers.

Tito adjusts her hand to get a new read and pushes his glasses up into a forehead wrinkle. "Talk about what?"

Teagan smacks her lips. "Whatever Allie may not want to say in front of you." Tito's dark cheeks redden.

Allie shakes her head. "It's okay. In fact, probably better for Tito to be part of this conversation."

Now Teagan is curious. *What is Allie up to?* She raises an eyebrow and waits for the other woman to speak.

Allie pulls at a piece of fuzz on her sleeve. "When the men jumped us, at the overpass . . . you didn't seem scared. I froze. I couldn't think of what to do. But you weren't frozen. You . . . *attacked* that man."

Teagan rolls her eyes. *Why is she so interested in this?* "I was defending myself. And protecting you, I might add. You're welcome for getting us both out of there alive."

Allie's brow creases. "Thank you?" She doesn't sound appreciative. She tells Tito, "I was frozen. You should have seen her . . . no hesitation at all."

Tito's eyebrows shoot up, dropping the glasses once again onto the bridge of his nose.

Teagan wonders if that hurts. She rolls her eyes. "I'm not a delicate flower. You both act as if women never defend themselves."

Their faces don't soften toward her. Allie shakes her head. "I was frozen."

Teagan looks skyward. "That's you. I'm me. What's the big deal?"

"Hey," Tito says. "Be still. I've got three more passes before you're done." He moves her hand to get a slightly different angle in the scan. "I can't believe you attacked someone."

That stings. Teagan shoots back, "You'd rather I be an octopus?"

Tito and Allie exchange a look.

"Are you two fucking or something?"

"What?" Tito's face is flushed.

Allie looks like she's bitten something tart. "No!"

"That's a relief," Teagan says. The pad chimes so she moves her hand before Tito can get to it. *Only one more after this.*

"Why would you think we're . . ." Tito can't bring himself to say the word.

"I don't know," Teagan says snidely, "you seem awfully chummy."

"This is ridiculous." Allie stands and impatiently adjusts her jacket. "We need to go see Carter."

Teagan's brow creases. "Why? Am I invited? Or do you mean just you and Tito?"

They exchange looks again and Teagan wants to thump them both. "Seriously? You had to think about that?" *What is going on here?*

The pad chimes. Teagan glances at Tito. He's completely forgotten about this task. She adjusts her hand on the pad for the final biometric scan. Allie's standing by the lab door. Teagan can't read her expression.

Allie calls the lab's Eye over to send a message. "Carter, this is Allie. You need to come down here. Tito and I need you to see something."

Tito's mouth falls open. "What the fuck, Allie?"

"Thank you!" Teagan says. "I was beginning to wonder whose side you were on."

Tito doesn't affirm her, however. He's still focused on Allie. "Why?"

"You know why," Allie says. "We talked about this."

"I'm still here!" The scanner beeps and Teagan is glad she's no longer stuck to the table. She leaps off and waves her hands. "Why are you talking about me like I'm not here? What's going on?"

"Teagan." Tito touches her shoulder. "Calm down."

"I am calm." That is true. She's speaking with heightened intention and volume, but it's not due to anger. "I'd just like to understand where Allie's sense of entitlement—and seeming authority—is coming from."

Carter strides into the lab. Teagan expects him to smile and greet them the way he always does. But his face looks pale and drawn. "What's going on here?"

Teagan jerks a thumb toward Allie. "This kid is a real button-pusher. I've tried to be nice, but . . ."

Carter raises his eyebrows. "I could say the same about you." He addresses Allie. "What did you want me to see?"

"You're seeing it."

Teagan doesn't like the way Allie looks at her. *Christ, the brass ovaries on this kid.* Although she does feel a twinge of envy. *I wish I had that kind of confidence at twenty-five.* "What is he supposed to see?"

Carter slides a hand down Teagan's arm. "You okay?"

"It's been a hell of a day," Teagan admits.

"She attacked someone," Allie adds.

Teagan nearly snaps her neck looking at Allie. "I was protecting us. Carter, we were attacked, and I defended us. We have a right to defend ourselves."

"Sure, sure," Carter says. He takes up Teagan's bandaged hand. "And you got hurt. Are you all right?"

Teagan exhales and realizes she's been holding her breath. *God, it's nice to have someone care for me.* "I must still be in shock because the pain hasn't kicked in, but I think I'll be fine. Tito bandaged me up."

Tito says, "Maybe you should kick off early?"

"I just got here," Teagan protests.

Carter frowns. "Teagan, you don't look well. Maybe Tito's right. You should go home, get some rest. Let's start fresh again tomorrow."

Both he and Tito look concerned. Teagan doesn't bother looking at Allie. *I've had enough of her today.* "What happened was pretty scary."

Tito nods. "Go home, get some rest."

Teagan hesitates. *What am I going to do at home all alone?*

As if Carter could hear her inner thoughts, he says, "Come over for dinner after work?"

"That sounds good." Teagan looks back at the lab table to make sure nothing fell out of her pockets. She pats her pants and feels the outline of her wallet. Keys are still in the purse in the Executive Suite, so she'll have to go up. *Have to call the car anyway.* Concern is etched across Tito and Carter's faces. She doesn't like seeing them worried about her, like she's some kind of weak link.

"Here," Carter says, heading to the lab door, "I'll see you out."

"Don't worry about it." She remembers to use her left hand for the security pad at the elevator. "See you at seven?"

Carter nods. "That works."

Teagan doesn't want to leave them, but she'd rather they talk behind her back than keep speaking in code in front of her. *Besides, Carter can't keep anything from me. I'll be able to figure out what Allie's up to at dinner.*

23

The console inside the elevator buzzes as soon as the doors close. It's a message from the Executive Suite Eye. Teagan activates the communication panel. "Yes?"

"Dr. McKenna, a visitor is waiting for you in the Executive Suite."

"Visitor?" This is unusual. Teagan doesn't recall anyone being on her calendar. The Eye is programmed to refuse any unscheduled guests.

Then, she remembers running into Roz in the lobby. *Maybe Ascha scheduled something?* But if Ascha wanted her to give a statement to *Humanity Now*, she would have called to go over the talking points first. "Who is it?"

"Special Agent Duncan Bridger."

Special Agent? "Is he FBI?"

"Affirmative. Pronouns are they/them. They say they're based at the Atlanta field office."

What business would a government agent have here? "Have you notified Carter and Tito?"

"Agent Bridger asked for you."

Teagan's mind whirls. "Did they state the purpose of their visit?"

"No."

This isn't the first time a government agent has visited NeuroNet. But usually, it's a legislator or someone from the Department of Defense.

FBI?

The doors open. Teagan can see the landing pad. *I could call the car and sneak out. Leave Tito and Carter to deal with the agent.* But she has to get the keys first. And they're in the Executive Suite.

Shit.

Reluctantly, she trudges into her office. Her desk is as clean as she left it, the night before Em's upload. *I never got a chance to mess it up before they decided to send me away.*

That thought rankles. *What is it about Allie?* She made an important discovery. She's a strong woman. Both things would endear her to Tito and Carter. *But it's like she's got some kind of power over them.* It doesn't make any sense at all.

A knock on the door interrupts her thoughts. "Dr. McKenna?"

The agent is tall and slender. There is something delicate about their nose and jawline. But a close-cropped beard keeps the face from looking too feminine. Teagan offers a chair and sits. "You must be Agent Bridger."

The agent smiles and unbuttons their jacket before sitting. They extract a digital pad from their pocket, tap it on, and remove its stylus. They look up at Teagan with a cocked head and bemused expression. "It's good to finally meet *the* Dr. Teagan McKenna."

Their flattering words somehow sound insulting. Teagan asks, "How may I help you, Agent Bridger?"

The Agent's smile twitches. "I was hoping you could shed some light on a little mystery."

"Mystery?" Teagan's brows knit as a series of mental alarm bells go off. *Does he mean the suicides?* She braces for questions about Em.

Instead, the agent says, "It's come to our attention that there's been an irregular pattern of Eye blackout requests in this suite. What can you tell me about that?"

Blackout requests? That doesn't seem worthy of an FBI inquest. *Unless...* Teagan searches her memories. Other than hacking into Dee Claybourne's background records, she can't think of anything illegal

Carter's done, and she's not going to voluntarily divulge that piece of information. "I don't know if I can tell you anything."

The agent leans forward. "Of course, any proprietary information specific to NeuroNet or trade secrets that might compromise your operations would remain safe with me."

"I'm sure," Teagan lies. "But I don't know if I can help you. You said there's an irregular pattern? What can you tell me about that?"

The agent frowns. For a minute Teagan wonders if they'll share anything. Then, they scroll down their pad. "You're aware that there are regulations on when an Eye may be put to sleep?"

"Of course. Carter and I are very aware. Have we been abusing the amount of time or frequency allotted to private businesses?"

"Not exactly." The agent cranes their slender neck until they identify the Eye's cradle. "Technically, you're not putting the Eye to sleep outside of the frequency or duration of time that you're allowed."

Teagan dislikes the wriggly way this agent operates. She prefers people to be direct. This agent's approach is wearing on her nerves. "So, it doesn't appear there's a problem here."

The agent's mouth twitches again. "Well . . . not with that, no."

Teagan can't help herself. She heaves a sigh. "Then, with what?"

The agent laughs. "I apologize. I know you're a remarkably busy woman."

"And I've had a long, exhausting day. You caught me as I was trying to take off early."

"I'm sure you're exhausted." They smile. "To tell you the truth, I didn't expect you back at work so soon after your wife's death."

Teagan freezes.

The agent continues. "I stopped by your house first, but the Eye told me you were here. I'm deeply sorry for your loss . . ."

"Thank you." She's not sure what they're playing at, but it makes her self-conscious, like she needs to explain or defend herself. "I realize most people wouldn't come back to the office so quickly, but . . ."

"But you're Dr. Teagan McKenna," the agent says with a smile and tone so sweet, they wouldn't melt butter, "and how could NeuroNet go on without you?"

She doesn't know if the agent is trying to be sincere or sarcastic. She opts to give them the benefit of the doubt. "That's right." Before they can reopen that line of thought, Teagan says, "You haven't answered my question, Agent Bridger. Why are you here investigating our blackout protocol if we haven't violated its terms?"

The agent crosses an ankle over their knee. "Dr. McKenna, does Dr. Carter Smith go home at night?"

"I don't snoop on him, but yes, I believe he does." Teagan's brows knit together. "Why do you ask?"

The agent turns his digipad around so she can see a graph on it. "This is a record of the blackout protocols enacted over the past week. Notice anything peculiar?"

Teagan takes the pad and examines the data. At first glance, she doesn't.

The agent prompts, "Look at the time stamps."

Teagan examines the stamps along the X axis and frowns. "They're at weird times."

"To put it mildly," the agent agrees. "Who else do you know who might be in your office between two and four o'clock in the morning?"

Maybe Tito? She suspects he lives in the lab. And he has security access to the Executive Suite. *But he could enact a blackout protocol downstairs. Why would he travel up here to turn the system off?* Teagan files the question away with the others she wants to ask Carter later tonight.

The agent's eyes remain fixed on her, but Teagan's decided not to share any information. If this were a serious matter, there would be more than one government agent here to take them all into custody. *Clearly, he's following a hunch. And hunches sometimes lead to dead ends.*

She smiles. "I'm sorry, Agent Bridger. I can't help you. As you know, I was out of the office during the dates in question, and I don't want to speculate. I'm a scientist. I prefer to deal with hard facts rather than conjecture or gossip. I'm sure you understand."

Bridger's thin lips purse. The agent doesn't look happy. But Teagan must have guessed right. They rise to leave. She tries not to smirk.

"A word of advice," Bridger says. "The Department of Defense is extremely interested in what you've developed here. As you can imagine, NeuroNet has useful real-world applications beyond the service you provide your customers. Some of my friends in the DOD are even working on use cases, if NeuroNet needs to be bailed out or . . ." The agent grins. ". . . taken over."

Teagan stiffens. *That's nothing to joke about.* She remembers when the Eyes were privately owned home assistants. They existed in multiple forms, offered by a variety of companies. Her own parents kept one in the kitchen to listen to music on. But after a massive, coordinated hack, the government consolidated ownership of the Eyes. Eyes became ubiquitous and more functional, but they also gave the government a window into your life.

Teagan knows how the government would utilize NeuroNet tech. And it wouldn't be for domestic use. The tech behind the AI-powered sexbots could easily be adapted to power non-human combat units. And why not upload world-class spies or government officials to preserve their wisdom and skill? Maybe they'd settle on one ruler they wanted to preside forever. She forces herself to smile. "If I think of anything, I'll let you know."

"Thank you," the agent says. They tap their pad and Teagan's console dings. "I've sent you my contact information should you need me."

She can't bring herself to thank him, so Teagan just nods.

24

It's magic hour—that gorgeous sunset-eve when everything glows rosy-gold. Few vehicles are in the air to obstruct Teagan's ride home. It's so beautiful, she wishes there were more cars to keep her suspended here. But it's time to descend.

Teagan pauses at the garage door. Like all the appliances within the house, this door is rose gold. *Em's color.* She lets it scan her irises and enters the kitchen. The austere whiteness of the counters and walls are cut through with slivers of rose gold. She drifts into the foyer. All the lamps, the ceiling fixtures, even the doorknobs are rose gold.

Em's touch is everywhere.

The doorbell rings. Teagan jumps. "Who on Earth?" The household Eye hovers over to relay the outdoor feed.

Aya's delicate face appears. "Can I come in?"

Teagan laughs, relieved. She issues the command and the door swings open. It's good to see Aya. *To have a friend.*

Teagan's mind glitches at that thought. She hadn't realized how lonely Tito and Carter's behavior made her feel. *Allie got to me more than I thought.* But Aya is here, waiting to be welcomed. Teagan smiles brightly. "To what do I owe the pleasure?"

"I stopped by the office to see you, but you had already left. I wanted to talk."

Teagan hugs her. "It's good to see you."

"I wish it were purely social, but . . ." Aya shrugs. "For people like us, work never really ends." She tilts her head, casting a glance around the foyer. "I like your home. It suits you: bright, stately, expansive."

Teagan laughs.

"What is so funny about that?"

"I was just noticing how much of Em is imprinted on this place. Like a gilded cage. It's funny you see me in it because I don't know if I can."

"Is it not your home? If you do not like what you see, change it."

Teagan looks at the entranceway with new eyes. She replaces all the rose-gold fixtures with blue-black metallic ones. In this way, the house becomes a temple of reason, filled with hard edges and clear thoughts. She smiles. *That is a change I'd like to see.*

Teagan asks, "Would you like something to drink?" She heads to the receiving room, where she keeps the bar cart.

Aya says, "Do you have green tea?"

Teagan reverses her trajectory and heads toward the kitchen. "I do."

Aya follows behind, laughter tinkling like a bell. "Did you think I would drink something harder?"

Teagan smirks over her shoulder. "Maybe?"

"Perhaps next time," Aya says. "I tried to call you at the office, but Tito said you had gone home. I hope you do not mind me following you here?"

"No . . ." To be honest, Teagan's not sure if she minds or not. She asks the Eye for green tea, and they settle into the breakfast nook. "What's going on?"

Aya leans forward and takes one of Teagan's hands. "I am worried about you."

Teagan laughs.

Aya frowns. "No. I mean it. I am worried about you. Have you used my headdress?"

Teagan's brows crease. Aya's always been intense, but this is extra, even for her. "Of course."

Aya raises her eyebrows. "How often?"

Teagan looks down. "Twice?"

"Teagan!"

Teagan holds up her hands. "I've been busy!"

Aya sighs. "That is not enough."

"What do you mean? Enough for what?"

"How are you feeling?"

"Fine, I think." Teagan doesn't like the waves of intent coming off Aya. "Everything seems kind of muffled in cotton since Em died. Has anyone you've loved ever died?"

Aya takes her time before saying, "My mother."

"How long did you grieve?"

"I was not raised with the same traditions as you. When my mother died, a bird took wing. I knew then that her soul had found another home."

The breeze knocks a dead branch against the window. Teagan jumps at the sound. Small funnels of wind-tossed dirt flay brown stalks of abandoned vines and withered rose bushes in the garden. Teagan asks Aya. "Do you think we are selfish, to want to keep people alive?"

Aya squeezes her hand. "Of course not. I thought what we set out to do with NeuroNet was beautiful. Noble, even."

"I thought so, too." Teagan frowns. "But since the Dee Claybourne incident, I've been rethinking that. And now with what happened to Em . . . I've been wondering if we should have interfered. Did we make things worse? We prevented loved ones from dying naturally. We kept their souls from finding another home."

"Who says the loved ones have no soul?" Aya tilts her head, eyes sparkling.

Not long ago this kind of attention would have lit Teagan up from top to tail. Maybe she's grown more comfortable with Aya. Perhaps she's matured. *Or maybe I'm still numb with grief. I don't feel a thing.* That is odd. And new. *Maybe this is how I will be now, for the rest of my life?*

"You worry so much about so many things," Aya says. "But death is part of life. Things end so they may begin again."

Teagan can't help scoffing. "That's not our business model."

Now it is Aya's turn to laugh. But it is a gentler sound. Like chimes in the wind. "Oh, Teagan, you see everything in such stark terms. There is no black and white. Yes, your loved ones pass through a death of the body, but their minds are reborn. They are not meant to be the same as they were. And that is what I tried to bring to NeuroNet. It is something Carter finally understands. To be fully alive, loved ones must be reborn and evolve into something else."

Teagan studies her friend. "Is that why you fought so hard to ungate the AI?"

Aya's lips turn down in thought. "I have grown old enough to question whether I was right about that."

Teagan smirks. "Is the great Dr. Aya Wakahisa admitting she was wrong?"

Aya rolls her eyes. "Still thinking in a binary. You are better than that, Teagan." She gazes back out at the garden. "You know the truth is always more complex than what is right and wrong. There are a million adjustments we can make during testing that will influence the outcome."

Teagan nods. "And sometimes no matter what we do, the outcome is the same." She gestures to the garden. "I don't know what I could have done to keep Em's garden alive. I tried."

"Perhaps you did not care enough."

"About Em?" Teagan feels like she should protest.

Aya shrugs one slender shoulder. "Does thinking that way upset you?"

"No." Teagan is surprised by what she really thinks. "Maybe I'm still in shock from this afternoon. Or grief . . ." A crow scratches at the base of a dead hydrangea bush. "If I'm to be honest. I don't miss Em anymore." She smiles at her friend. "And I don't feel guilty saying that."

Aya nods. "It is better to let life wash over us. To feel what we feel without judging our thoughts. If we try holding on too tightly, we might get pulled under or fall behind."

Teagan smiles. She wants to let Aya wash over her. But that is irresponsible. "All right, if you're going to get existential on me, I'm going to have a real drink." Teagan waves down the Eye. "Do you want something stronger than tea?"

"No."

Teagan frowns. As much as she loves Aya, Teagan hates games. "Why are you here, Aya?"

Aya folds her delicate fingers on the table in front of her. "Tell me about this afternoon. What happened?"

"Carter and Tito didn't brief you?"

"They did, but I want to hear from you, in your own words, without their interpretations."

Teagan nods. The Eye deposits a scotch by her elbow, and she gratefully takes a sip. "I wanted to get to know the new lab assistant, Allie, so I invited her out to lunch—"

"What do you think of her?"

Teagan winces. "Honestly? Not a fan."

"Why? Tito says she made an important breakthrough."

Teagan scoffs, "It wasn't anything I couldn't have discovered."

"But you did not. You were distracted. By Em perhaps?"

"Maybe. That doesn't stop her from being annoying. She acts like she owns the place."

Aya chuckles. "Maybe she will, one day."

"Don't say, 'There's no ceiling for a woman with ambition,' because you and I know that's hooey."

Aya shrugs. "I do not feel like I have reached my ceiling yet, have you?"

"No." Teagan sips her whiskey and shoots Aya an annoyed look.

Aya touches the bandage over Teagan's right hand. "Did Allie do this?"

Teagan laughs. "I wish. Then I'd have a reason to hate her. No. I . . . lunch was okay. I enjoyed talking with her. She's got a good mind.

She's funny. If anyone but Carter and Tito introduced her to me, I'd probably really like her."

"That is big of you to admit."

"I'm not an asshole. I'm human."

Aya raises her eyebrows. "So, what happened?"

"Some guys followed us. Threatened us . . . Allie wasn't much help, but I hurt one. That was why we were able to get away." Allie's reaction still puzzles Teagan. "But for some reason, Allie not only wasn't grateful that I got us out of there, but she also acted like I must be crazy. I don't get it."

Aya's small mouth purses. "What happened to your hand?"

Teagan looks at the bandage. Tito wrapped it well. "The weapon I found was a piece of glass. I cut my palm, but you should have seen the other guy." She doesn't mean to laugh, but the memory of his eyeball bouncing from a strand of nerve is too absurd. She can't help herself.

Aya frowns. She extends her hand. "May I see the damage?"

Teagan's laughter dries up. "I don't know if I have any bandages to redress the wound. I don't want to get it infected."

Aya nods. "Understandable. But I brought something with me."

Reluctantly, Teagan lets Aya unwrap the bandage. The gash is deep, but it's no longer bleeding. Aya extracts a slender vial from her purse and brushes some of its liquid across Teagan's palm.

Teagan snaps to attention. She recognizes the vial. It's acid—the same thing Allie tried to hand Tito in the lab. "What are you . . .?" She jerks back, but Aya won't release her. Teagan stares at the drops of acid. Then, at the chemical reaction racing across the gash on her palm.

Her mind races. *This isn't what acid does to skin.*

Aya's expression is inscrutable.

This is how you repair a Model Two shell. Teagan's wound has vanished. "Aya . . . am I . . . did they . . .?"

Teagan's mind whirls. *What am I?*

Teagan's chair clatters to the floor as she stands. "Aya. What did they do to me?"

Aya stows the vial away in her purse.

She knew what to bring. She knows I'm no longer human. How?

Aya answers Teagan's unspoken question. "I was on your upload team."

"You uploaded me? That's impossible. That's illegal!"

"Will you please sit?" Aya's lips press into a thin purple line. "It hurts my neck to look up at you, and we have so much to discuss."

Teagan wants to refuse, but what good would that do? She rights the chair and sits.

"Tito and Carter called me in a panic. Your vitals were crashing. We had to act fast. You were hemorrhaging. Luckily, we were able to extract you."

"Lucky for who?" *I'm an upload?* Teagan pinches herself to see if she's dreaming. But it doesn't hurt. *Shit.* "I'm an upload."

"Would you rather be dead?"

"I'd rather you didn't lie to me." Teagan replays the events of the past few days since she woke up in the hospital. "I'm not numb with grief. I'm numb cause I'm dead? How long were you all going to lie to me?"

"Technically, I am the only one who is not lying to you," Aya says. "Tito could have healed you, but he chose not to."

"The vial." Allie tried to hand Tito a vial like that in the lab. *Why? Because she knew it would fix my hand?* "Oh my God," Teagan says, piecing it together. "Allie . . . She knows?"

"Yes."

"Why the hell would Tito and Carter trust her?"

Aya's eyebrows rise. "Are you jealous?"

Teagan can't meet her gaze. "Can robots get jealous?" Fat droplets of rain are beginning to fall. One hits the crow's beak. It squawks at the injustice before taking wing.

Aya tsks. "You know you are not a robot."

"What am I?" Teagan touches her cheek and is shocked to find liquid there. She holds the synthetic tear up to Aya. "This situation frustrates me. Tears form. But I'm not feeling anything. These aren't real tears.

This body is simulating reality, but it's a lie. I'm not here, in this body, feeling frustration."

"Then where are you, Teagan?" Aya cocks her head. "Not dead. Not gone. Not forgotten." She touches Teagan's hand.

"I don't know," Teagan answers honestly. "I can't believe you had to tell me. I knew something was off. The way the boys were acting . . . And Allie? I'm such an idiot."

Aya shrugs. "The human mind sees what it wants to see and nothing else." She traces a line across Teagan's palm. "Yes, your mind tricked you. It did not have all the data it needed to reach the right conclusion. But now you know. And something else you should know: you are different from the others."

"Thank you?" Teagan's mind reels. "It's good I can't feel rage."

"Yes, I imagine it is." Aya sits back and sips her tea.

Reflexively, Teagan picks up her scotch and sips it. She laughs, staring into its caramel depths. "What a waste of good scotch. I might as well be drinking motor oil."

"You know that would not break down properly," Aya says, ignoring Teagan's joke. "At least, by drinking good scotch, you are creating fuel for your body."

"I meant that it's wasted on me." Teagan frowns. "It doesn't matter what I'm drinking. I can't taste it. I can't enjoy it."

Aya arches an eyebrow. "Do you need to taste something to enjoy it?"

"What a stupid question."

"I do not think it is stupid. I am serious. You have been in the body for several days. Have you found anything pleasurable?"

Teagan scrolls through what she's done since 'waking' in the hospital. "I had a nice night with Carter. That felt . . . normal."

"The memory of something pleasurable can be as nice as the thing itself."

Teagan is tired of this. "Aya, why did you come over?"

Aya shrugs. "Tito said you attacked someone. Carter and Allie think you are in danger of hurting yourself . . . or others."

Teagan raises an eyebrow.

Aya laughs. "Mainly they fear you hurting others. You were aggressive with the man on the street and with the protestors."

"I'm not crazy. I acted out of self-defense." Teagan slumps back in her chair and stares at the ceiling. "God! What did they expect me to do? Just stand there and take abuse?"

"Is that not what you normally would have done?"

Teagan stares at Aya, mouth agape. But Aya's face remains placid. Teagan realizes Aya is not accusing her.

The truth lands on Teagan. "Shit. Yes. Yes. It is. I would have frozen up, gotten hurt . . . let them hurt me . . ." She puts her head in her hands. *"Shit."*

Aya's voice is gentle. "That is why Carter and Tito are scared. You are evolving. That means your behavior is no longer something they can predict."

Teagan scoffs. "I can't evolve. That's not . . ." She lets the thought trail off as she remembers something Aya said. "*You* were on the upload team?"

Aya nods. "It does not scare me. Your evolution."

Teagan studies her friend's impassive face. "Aya . . . did Carter let you ungate my AI?"

Aya sips her tea.

Teagan reminds her, "It's a simple question." A wry thought crosses her mind. "You know, the old me would be fuming by now. Does that mean I'm evolving into a better person?"

"You are evolving. I hope into someone better than you were." Aya looks off toward the garden. The rain churns the earth, transforming dust into mud. "You used the headdress?"

"Yes. But I don't know that it did anything."

Aya points over Teagan's shoulder at the greatest hits slideshow of young, happy Teagan and young, happy Em. Teagan's not sure what Aya's trying to say. Aya cocks her head, reminding Teagan of the crow. "What do you think of when you see those pictures?"

Teagan watches the images spool past. Knowing that she's no longer human is liberating, in a way. Teagan can hold the horror of what's happened to her in her mind. She can see it for what it is and name it. She should have died. Her body should have been buried. Well, the physical part probably is. But, people should have mourned her, then moved on.

She contemplates the crime Aya, Tito, and Carter committed. Her best friends, most intimate companions—none of whom had a legal right to do so—took it upon themselves to extend her life. They extracted her consciousness, uploaded it to the NeuroNet, downloaded it into a synthetic body, and then let her believe she was still human. But this is not what Aya asked her to consider.

Teagan refocuses on the slideshow. "What do I see? I see how happy we were. How much we loved each other. Once. That much is obvious. I can't believe how little all that love meant after a while. It's sad, really." She turns back to Aya. "You know, Em was always jealous of you."

The corner of Aya's mouth twitches. "Why? We were never lovers."

"I respected you in a way I couldn't respect her," Teagan says. "You excited me in a way that she didn't anymore."

"Why do you think that is?"

Teagan considers the question. "Without trust, there can't be true intimacy. Love is built on intimacy and trust. We weren't intimate, you and I, physically. But I trusted you. I loved you as a friend."

"Loved?" Aya raises her eyebrows.

"Maybe not so much in the past tense," Teagan admits. "There was a part of me that wanted to be with you."

"I know."

Teagan is surprised by Aya's response.

But what Aya says next surprises her even more. "And that may be possible later. But first there are things for you to do."

"Like what?" Aya is silent. "Does this have to do with the head-dress?" Aya nods. Teagan signals the Eye to fetch it. She fingers the delicate box. "What was this supposed to do?"

Aya's mouth purses. "What it has done," she corrects, "is neutralize negative thought patterns and coax you toward finding more positive solutions."

Teagan's brows knit. "You think it worked?"

"You chose a different method of defense when you were attacked. Your actions prevented you from being harmed." Aya's smile looks sad. "Your reaction was violent but effective. And the outcome was far better than what would have happened if you had frozen up, like Allie."

"I know!" *Finally! Someone who gets it.* "Why did that scare Tito and Carter?"

"You need to ask them about that," Aya says, walking to the sink.

"You're kidding, right?" Teagan follows her.

Aya washes out her cup. "Of course not, you have a dinner date with Carter, do you not?"

Teagan frowns.

Aya dries the teacup and places it on the counter with precision and care. Her eyes no longer sparkle. They are dark, solemn pools. Aya sighs and says, "They want to deactivate you, Teagan."

Teagan inhales sharply. "They wouldn't!"

Aya dries her hands. "They fear what you are capable of. I am not. I have faith in you. In your ability to see clearly and do what you need to do."

Something in Aya's manner is so intent, Teagan gets the feeling there's something important lurking behind Aya's words. Teagan wants to know what she's not saying. "What do I need to do?"

Aya neatly folds and replaces the hand towel. "If you do not go to dinner, they will deactivate you. If you go, you might be able to prevent that."

"How?"

"I cannot tell you that. But I can tell you something that will help."

Teagan raises her eyebrows. "Okay. Shoot."

"There are questions you need to answer. And you—out of all of us —are best positioned to discover the answers. Why did Dee Claybourne kill herself? What happened between you and Em? Is there a way to keep NeuroNet bots from self-destructing or harming others? Once you know the answers to those questions, I have faith you will know exactly what to do."

"Seriously?" Teagan's mouth twists. "You think I haven't been thinking about that already?" She shakes her head. "That's all I've been thinking about for the past couple of months."

"No." Aya's eyes soften. "No, you have not. You have been distracted. Now you know the truth about yourself, there is nothing left to distract you. Use the headdress. Meditate on the questions. Go to Carter and see if he can be moved. I do not want to see you destroyed. Convince him that you deserve to live."

"He can't honestly want to be rid of me." Teagan scoffs. But the look in Aya's eyes convinces her otherwise.

"Promise me you will use the headdress. Consider the questions and all the options that come to you."

Aya offers her hand in parting. Teagan takes it. It's an absurdly old-fashioned gesture. Teagan replies with an equally archaic response. She bows deeply to kiss Aya's hand. "I promise."

25

Teagan pulls a chair in front of the kitchen window. Meditation—actually, reflection of any kind—has never been her thing. She prefers clear thought followed by clean action. *But I made a promise. So, head-dress it is.* And isn't meditation supposed to be amplified by nature?

Not that the garden offers much. In its brittle, broken, brown, and muddy state it's not very inspiring. But it's hers now, and she'll be able to choose what to do with the space to make it her own later.

If I get to live that long.

The thought is sobering.

Enough delay. Put the damn headdress on and see what it does with those dark thoughts!

Teagan smiles at the impatient little voice in her head and opens the box. The headdress shimmers. It is exactly the kind of thing she'd expect Aya to create. It's delicate, gorgeous, and trembling with promise. She lifts it to the crown of her head, settles it down, and switches it on. It hums to life.

Instantly, Teagan feels a ripple of warm energy cascade through her body. *Did it feel this way before?* She can't remember. She closes her eyes and concentrates on the sensations. The pulsation is soft and rhythmic. Soothing. She can feel the pace of her thoughts slow. The pulse reminds her of a stop-action film that played in biology class when she was in ninth grade. It showed them how a fern grew. It's a funny thing to remember now. She's not sure why she's thinking of it, but something in the comparison feels right to her, so she latches onto the image. Her consciousness is a little green question mark, moving like a new fern frond. It's emerging from its hidden home in the dark core of the NeuroNet. It pokes up bravely, nosing its way into the sunshine of the pleasant waves emitted by the headdress. The fuzzy spiral of her thoughts absorbs the warmth. Her mind unfurls in the slowest, most luxurious way. She feels tendrils of thought reaching out, hitting the limit of their fullest expression and then evolving . . .

Oh. This is the dangerous part . . . my capacity to evolve . . . to be more than who I was. She begins to retreat, away from the unfurling.

Who says this is dangerous? Maybe this is who you were always meant to become?

Teagan considers both sides and reaches a conclusion. *If they're going to disconnect me anyway, what do I have to lose? Might as well push the limits and see what I'm capable of.*

She recalls what she knows about artificial intelligence. If she's ungated, then her thoughts are spiraling out, capturing new inputs, and then using that information to leap out into another spiral.

Am I still me? Teagan knows the old Teagan is still within arm's reach. But now that she knows what she is and what must be happening, she can see the ways in which she's changing. Ways that she is fracturing the chokeholds of past conditioning. *This impulse to try new things isn't simple curiosity. It's a drive to improve, to evolve.*

The proof is in her behavior. What's better than being abused? *Fighting back.* What's better than being stuck? *Leaping into the unknown.*

No wonder Carter and Tito are terrified. If Teagan were human, she'd be horrified, too. She's an unnatural being with unlimited potential. And not only is it a strong possibility that her personality will change, there's also no way to predict if she'll be a good or bad android once she does.

"God, as if being a woman weren't complex enough." She laughs.

She can hear Aya's voice in her head: *Enough. You have work to do.*

She enjoys being pushed and nudged. Teagan smiles. Time to put her processing power to effective use.

She focuses on Tito's saying. *Don't die like an octopus, die like a hammerhead shark.*

So, if Allie's right, the dissonant actions we're seeing—the death urge—is being driven by a resistance to death.

That doesn't make sense.

If you didn't want to die, then you'd preserve your own life at all costs.

Unless living is worse . . .

The central question was: why would someone given the gift of eternal life want to end their own?

But what if that's the wrong question?

What is the right question?

Maybe: is it better to die a natural death than live an unnatural life?

Dee Claybourne thought so. So did Jethro. Em did not. She wanted to live at all costs.

What do I want?

Teagan realizes with a jolt that this is the first time she has ever asked herself that question. There is another question she's also never asked.

What do I need?

She wondered about Em's needs all the time. About NeuroNet, Carter, Tito—anyone and everything in her life has been the focus of her attention at some point and time. Sometimes to an obsessive level.

But did I ever think about myself, my needs?

Em always accused Teagan of being selfish, but how could she have been selfish if she never knew what she genuinely wanted or needed? Teagan shakes her head and sheds that guilt. It's no longer useful.

She considers what another motivating factor might be.

Fear.

That's important.

What do I fear?

That is easy to answer.

"I fear fucking up. Failing everyone. Letting them down."

That is a human feeling, though. *Do I still care about that?* She probes the edges of her mind.

No.

The fear is gone. Guilt is gone.

What do I want and need?

She's no longer human, at least not flesh and blood human. At her core, though, she remembers what everything felt like. She remembers joy. She can imagine it in her body. Same with hunger. And desire. She can no longer taste salt, but she remembers the feel and taste of it on her tongue, and the difference between licking it off a bagel, the rim of a shot glass, and her lover's stomach.

With interest, Teagan notes that her synthetic body is responding to her thoughts. Her nipples are hard. She feels moisture between her legs. She smirks. "Good engineering."

She feels an urge to receive, to give love. She quiets her thoughts and focuses on the ripples of sensation radiating from the crown of her head, mingling with the coiled snake in her belly, and lets them sync with each other. *This must be what Em found. This pleasure.*

It's not life. It's life-like. A simulation.

But I am feeling. I am learning. An Albert Einstein quote springs to mind, "Once you stop learning, you start dying."

Do other bots have the capacity to learn?

No.

Am I sure?

If they had never attempted suicide before, Dee and Jethro learned how after they were uploaded.

But was that a learned response?

What's the alternative?

Was that a behavioral response? A rebellion? She thinks of octopi and hammerhead sharks again. Teagan imagines how trapped she felt in her marriage to Em. *And I had the freedom to leave. How oppressive would it have been knowing I was captive to her whims?*

That's a possibility. If Teagan were dying of an incurable disease, she would have begged Em to let her die. *What if Em ignored my wishes and I found myself brought back to life?*

And that's exactly what Carter, Tito, and Aya did. Could that be why I attacked the sandy-haired man?

Could that have been why Dee Claybourne and Jethro Nolan killed themselves: a built-up frustration of being uploaded against their will, frozen in amber, and caught in a body that would never age?

Is that what causes violence?

And if they felt no pleasure . . . if they only could remember what life was like, without being able to live it . . .

That could be its own soul-deadening practice.

Teagan thinks of Em. Em enjoyed the sensations. Without ego, Teagan reflects on their relationship. *I could not give Em what she needed. And I was too selfish to let her go. I wanted to possess her. That's not a healthy way to love.*

Teagan doesn't think Em meant to die. *She just wanted to be free of me.*

Pushing Teagan down the stairs then was not a well-thought-out action, even though Em always had been impulsive.

Now, I understand her frustration. I should have let her take lovers and taken my own. What would it have harmed? I couldn't love her. Why shouldn't she find enjoyment elsewhere?

Teagan sees how much ego chained them both. Kept them from forming healthier patterns and relationships. It wasn't just Em who couldn't evolve . . . *I was stuck in my own habits.*

She and Carter started NeuroNet to keep loved ones together forever. *But are we meant to love someone forever?*

Teagan's not sure how much love is involved in the desire to upload. *It's a wanting. People want to keep things the same. They want to keep loved ones by their side. So nothing has to change.*

Want is different from need. People need water to live. They don't need love. Or even companionship.

She opens her eyes. The garden is dead. But its decay holds the promise of new life. Spring always follows winter. Things grow, ripen, and die. Without that death, there can be no renewal. Living things need that pause. They need to grieve, let go, and keep growing.

We don't allow for growth. And growth is life.

So, who does the NeuroNet serve?

It doesn't make loved ones happy.

Does it make guardians happy?

Is Carter happy holding on to the memory of his dead child? Does it help or hurt his growth to have Rhys beside him as a constant reminder of what was?

One thing is certain: NeuroNet makes a lot of money.

But did that make me, Tito, or Carter happy?

She thinks of the FBI agent. If the government finds out that she's been uploaded, what would they do? *Steal our tech? Weaponize it?*

That can't happen.

It's only a matter of time. And if I'm deactivated, no one living will know how to do the right thing.

Teagan sighs. She knows what she needs to do. But she doesn't know how.

The crow is back, scratching at the ground. It finds a treasure and extracts it.

She hopes she can do the same.

26

The headdress remains in a box on Teagan's kitchen counter, but Teagan can still feel phantom traces of its pulsating warmth trickling through her system. The best science is like magic. *And if that headdress can produce sensations in me, then Aya's created some powerful magic.*

Teagan checks the time on the car dashboard. She'll arrive at Carter's house soon. The rain eclipsed the sunset, but the first stars are bravely cutting through the fog. It's not magic hour, but there's beauty in this transition, too.

Teagan laughs. It appears Aya's headdress is turning her into a romantic. *Next I know, I'll be finding beauty in everything.* The thought of being a sentimental android tickles her funny bone.

She's still laughing as the car descends to land on Carter's carport.

She could ring the bell, but she's curious to see if Carter's changed his security settings, so she lets the pad outside scan her retinas. The front door swings open with a satisfying click. *Either he still trusts me, or he's too preoccupied to care about his own security.*

The layout of Carter's home is like her own. She suspects he used her home as inspiration for his custom-remodel, although she's never confirmed it. She bypasses the dining room and heads to the kitchen. She didn't get a chance to say hello to Carter's dog Charlie last time she was here. The pitiful thing is so old he rarely rises from his bed.

If this is my last night on Earth, I want to say goodbye to all my old friends.

The kitchen is as she remembers it, but Charlie's bed is gone. She hears footsteps and whirls to see Carter in the doorway.

"Teagan?" Carter is smiling, but Teagan can see panic in his eyes.

This was a miscalculation. I'm supposed to put him at ease. Instead, I'm acting weird. She smiles. "Sorry, I wanted to say 'hi' to Charlie. Did you move his bed?"

Carter's eyes are wet. "Oh . . ."

She understands now why there's no dog bed here. "Oh shit. Did he . . . die?"

Carter nods. Teagan wraps her arms around him. "I'm so sorry." She feels him tense, but she holds the hug until he gives in. "When? Why didn't you tell me?"

"You were dealing with Em, and . . . To be honest, I can't talk about it without . . ." Tears choke him.

Teagan strokes his hair. "Shh . . . It's okay. I get it. Damnit. He was such a sweet dog."

Carter wipes the corner of his eye. "He was."

"Is Rhys okay?"

"Oh . . ." He waves his hand vaguely. "She loved him, but you know . . ."

Teagan nods, but inside, a snide little voice is chuckling. *Yeah, I know, bots can't feel. We're not human.* Thinking of herself as an upload is still an uncomfortable thing. But she's growing accustomed to it. It no longer seems a stigma. *Soon, I may think of it as an advantage.*

He tells the Eye to bring them drinks. "How are *you* doing?"

Teagan shrugs and swallows the first thing she wants to say. It's too sharp. Instead, she decides to play at being human a little longer. "Not sure. This afternoon really threw me for a loop."

Carter nods. "You've been through a lot. You should maybe take the rest of the week off."

Teagan bristles. "Are you trying to get rid of me?" It sounds more bitter than she means it to.

He laughs, but it is a shocked, mirthless sound. "Of course not."

The Eye deposits drinks on the table. Teagan takes hers and sits. The lights in Carter's garden flicker on. They must be on a timer. Melody didn't bother with rose bushes or things you had to baby. She planted solid hedges and fruit trees. Even in the winter, it's green. The hedges are blooming. The lights dance off a sea of white flowers and highlight abstract statuary standing sentinel over the compact space.

"Everything Em planted is dead. Maybe I should put hedges in like you did. What are they?"

"Camellias." Carter smiles. "And they smell great, too."

Teagan nods. "I like how they bloom during the winter."

Carter sits across the table from her. "Melody knew what she was doing. They bloom from November to April. As soon as the white ones die back, there's a sea of red ones that pop out."

"I miss her."

Carter nods "I miss her, too."

The sound of tiny footsteps draws their attention to the doorway. "Auntie Teagan!" Rhys claps her hands and runs to them. Teagan opens her arms to scoop the child up, but as soon as her hands meet the child's shoulder, she feels a shock of electricity.

"Are you okay?" Carter asks.

Teagan looks at Rhys. The child's eyes are wide. "Yeah," Teagan says, and wonders: *why does electricity arc between bots? Are we not grounded?*

If electricity can travel between us, what else might be transferred? "Come here, Rhys." She holds out her hand and braces for the current to connect.

Now that she expects it, Teagan welcomes the shock. She imagines following the spark as it arcs from her body to Rhys's.

For a moment, their hands connect and hold, like something magnetic. Rhys's eyes go wide. She pulls back, but Teagan won't release her.

Not until I know.

Teagan gathers up a piece of herself and tries to force it through their joined hands from her body into Rhys's. She isn't sure if it worked, but she can't hold on to Rhys any longer without creeping both Rhys and Carter out. She releases the child.

Did it work?

Teagan blinks. She can't focus her eyes. She blinks again and then realizes it's not the focus that's the problem. What she's experiencing is double vision.

Rhys blinks rapidly, rubbing her eyes.

Can she see out of my eyes, too? Teagan wonders if the child will be able to figure out what happened. *I think our consciousnesses are joined.*

Carter extends a hand toward Rhys. "Are you okay?"

Teagan holds her breath, but the child responds, "Yes, Daddy." Carter goes to order another drink from the Eye.

Teagan leans down and whispers, "You see what I see and what you see?" Teagan watches understanding dawn across the child's face. "We're connected."

The child frowns. "What?"

It's not safe to say more than that out loud. Their connection hangs in the air, like an invisible thread. Teagan sends a feeler down it until she finds the part of her consciousness lodged in Rhys's body. She thinks down that passageway, *We're connected.*

The child's mouth falls open.

Teagan thinks at her again: *Nod if you can hear me.*

Rhys nods once, curls bouncing.

Good. The double-vision perspective makes it hard to think. *Stand by my side. If we face the same way, it will be easier to process what we see.*

The child feels around the edge of the table until she can grab Teagan's hand. Teagan smiles down at her. To reduce the disorientation of both, she closes her eyes and sees just through the child's. As unflattering as the angle is, Teagan is shocked by how young she appears. Clearly this is the body they made for the Model Two launch. If Teagan spent any time in front of a mirror she would have noticed. *Twelve years is a long time. I didn't realize how old I got.*

Rhys tugs at her arm. "Auntie Teagan? Where is Auntie Em?"

"Oh." She steals a glance at Carter. He shakes his head. *He doesn't want me to say anything.*

"Say what?" Rhys asks.

Carter's brows furrow. "What?"

"Oh." Teagan didn't realize Rhys could hear her thoughts when she wasn't trying. *But of course, she can.* If they're entangled and can see through each other's eyes why wouldn't they have access to each other's data and communication systems? "Sorry we didn't tell you sooner, sweetie. We had to put Auntie Em to sleep."

Rhys's eyes look wet, but Teagan knows it's programming. The digital connection to sad news has been made and now the behavioral reaction is in play. "She's . . . sleeping?"

It takes a nanosecond for Teagan to recall this is how Carter explained Melody's death to the child. "Yes . . . Auntie Em is sleeping."

Rhys nods. "Like Charlie."

"Exactly like Charlie," Carter says, sounding proud of the child's association.

But he can't see the memories Rhys is reviewing, not like Teagan. These are recent ones. *When did Charlie die?*

Not die, the child's thoughts are sharp. *Sleeping. I put him to sleep.*

You? She feels a slight wary prickle at the base of her spine. *How did you put him to sleep?*

Daddy pills, Rhys answers silently and Teagan can see how the child crushed them and mixed them into Charlie's wet food dinner. "He doesn't feel any pain anymore," Rhys explains with pride.

Carter nods, pleased. "That's right. When you go to sleep, you don't have to worry about pain anymore."

"Or being sad," Rhys adds. "When you don't enjoy life, it's better to sleep."

"That's right, sweetie," Carter says.

Daddy's sad, Rhys thinks to Teagan. *He needs sleep.*

The child has a plan. She shares it with Teagan. It's very clever. It will work. Rhys wants it to work. She wants to do this soon. She thinks it will help.

"No." Teagan blurts out. "Don't think so."

Carter's laugh sounds nervous.

Teagan didn't mean to speak aloud. The last thing she wants to do is freak Carter out. But she's so shocked by Rhys's line of logic and the glimpse she's received of the child's well-thought-out plan . . . She takes a breath and thinks, urgently: *Do NOT put your Dad to sleep.*

Rhys pouts. Teagan remains firm with her. *He needs another kind of rest. He's under a lot of pressure, but he's not in serious pain.*

Carter squeezes Teagan's hand. "You think Em is in a better place now?" His eyes search her face. "Now that she's . . . sleeping?"

Teagan contemplates the question. On the surface, it is a great relief to be free of Em. Teagan is sure she would have grieved the loss of her love longer under different circumstances. It was cruel of her friends to let her think her numbness was grief.

Did he invite me over to come clean? If he did, Teagan would play dumb. She won't make this easy for him. She'll make him squirm a little before she lets him know she knows the truth, too.

Carter's eyes are puffy with drink. He's beginning to get jowls. He's clearly not taking care of himself.

Does he look at himself at all? Or does he depend on us to reflect to him who he is?

That's a scary thought. *Especially if we're not changing. He will keep getting older and sicker while we stay the same.*

She thinks about Rhys's plan. *Poor Carter, even the things we love are trying to destroy us.*

She ignores Rhys's protest against that thought and tells him, "You don't look well."

"You changed the subject."

"Sorry." Teagan realizes he's still waiting for an answer. "I'm sure Em isn't conscious of where she is now, so how could it matter?"

She ignores Rhys's question about dreams and smiles at Carter. "Should we eat?"

Carter's brows furrow. Teagan tries to smile even sweeter. She doesn't like this game. She'd rather be direct. But if he doesn't know she's off, then she's safe from being deactivated. Right? Might as well continue the charade. And dinner would be next, normally.

He stands. "Sure. Let's eat."

Teagan touches his elbow. "I'm really sorry about Charlie, I know you loved that dog."

"Thanks." There are tears in his eyes. She wraps her arm around him. It's disorienting seeing what she sees while also seeing through Rhys's eyes. She focuses on one of Carter's eyes and hopes she doesn't look crazy.

Is Daddy crying?

Yes. Teagan considers stepping to the side so Rhys can get a better view before realizing she already has one—through Teagan's eyes. The child's mind is racing. Teagan tries to put some distance between Rhys's thoughts and her own. But it's difficult.

They round the corner. Allie is sitting at the dining room table.

Teagan's mouth falls open. "What the fuck, Carter?"

"Language," he says, darting his eyes toward Rhys.

Teagan is done playing. "What the hell is Allie doing here?"

"Auntie Allie lives with us," Rhys says.

Teagan takes a second to process that. "She . . . what?" That doesn't make any sense.

But it's obviously true—Teagan can see the memories and hear the child thinking about her. Rhys likes her—a lot.

Teagan grips her head, but that doesn't make Rhys's thoughts any quieter. With effort, she manages to stutter out: "Will someone please tell me what is going on?"

Allie stands and waves her in. "I will."

Teagan's mouth drops open. "Anyone but her?"

Allie and Carter exchange glances. Teagan waves a hand in front of her friend's face. "I'm right here."

Allie sighs heavily. "I was hoping Carter was telling you in the kitchen. That's what I sent him in there to do." She narrows her eyes, shakes her head, and sits.

Teagan raises her eyebrows. She's not going to ask again. She knows they heard her. Besides, Rhys's thoughts are getting louder. It takes a lot of energy for Teagan to block them out. Her limbs are becoming difficult to maneuver forward. She pulls out a chair to sit. The simple gesture seems to take much longer than she's used to. She sits, propping her chin in her hands so she doesn't have to waste energy holding her head up. *Why am I so tired?* "Go on. I'm listening . . .," she says.

Allie smiles. "Good. Because if you weren't, it'd be a pity. As it is, you're already a waste."

Waste? Of what? Time? Money? Resources? Allie's choice of words reinforces what Teagan suspects: *She knows and considers me an experiment of some kind.* Teagan remains silent. *Don't make it easy for them.*

But Allie doesn't seem to struggle to express herself. In fact, she appears relieved to be telling Teagan hard news. Her words flow like water: "Carter and Tito couldn't bear to let you die. But they didn't want to make the same mistakes they made with Em. If there was any chance of discovering how to fix this issue we're having with outliers like Dee, Jethro, and Em, then it would be irresponsible not to take it. That's why the boys asked Aya to assist with the upload."

Boys. Allie called Carter and Tito 'boys.' Allie thinks of them as *her* boys.

The realization is cold and hard. *I think of them as my boys.*

Teagan looks at Allie. She thinks about all the things that bothered her about this woman before—how close Allie appeared to Tito and Carter, how she and Allie share the same humor, how she seemed to know all the executive team inside jokes. She's a mirror image of Teagan —not physically, but . . .

Oh shit.

Teagan swings for the fences when she asks, "Allie . . . is that Allie for the Alpha test?" Teagan hopes she'll strike out. But she can tell before Allie speaks that instead, she's hit a home run.

"Yes. I'm the original upload of your—our—consciousness. Aya insisted we also have a Beta test with an ungated operating system. To make it as useful as possible, they housed your consciousness in a body modeled on us. In an ideal world, it would be age-appropriate, but no one expected us to die." She laughs.

Teagan doesn't join her. "No, no one did. I know I didn't. Thanks for being honest with me." Her mind spins out: *Why tell me if they're going to deactivate me? Why not just pull the plug? Maybe there's a chance they won't?* Something like hope flares up within her.

Allie clucks. "I'm sure you've already figured it out and were just playing dumb. I felt bad not telling you before, making you jealous, but I didn't want to skew the results."

"And they're too skewed now?" Teagan grabs Rhys's hand. She's exhausted from maintaining a presence in both bodies.

But if they tried to deactivate this shell, maybe I could join Rhys in hers?

Teagan decides to stall. She asks Allie, "Is that why you reacted so strongly to my attempt to defend us? Because it's not like us to fight back?"

Allie's eyes flick to Carter before she answers. Teagan doesn't have the energy to look at him. She knows how he'll look: sweaty, bloated, nervous, and ashamed. *Good. That's how he should feel.*

Allie leans forward. "You know what concerns us: why would anyone who's been given the gift of eternal life throw it away? But that's not our only problem. We have a new one—one that both Em and you have highlighted–what happens when a bot acts out? Why would those who love us want to cause us harm? How can we predict and prevent that from happening?"

Teagan can hear Rhys's tiny voice in her head. It sounds almost remorseful: *I just wanted Daddy to feel better. But, that would have harmed him?*

Yes, Teagan thinks.

Oh, Rhys replies. *That was wrong.*

Teagan looks at Rhys. *She's gated, but she learned. That's amazing!* "They're capable of learning right from wrong," she tells Allie. "We don't have to deactivate the bots. We can teach them."

"If we had the time," Allie says, "that would be a perfect solution."

Teagan's brow furrows. "What do you mean 'if we had the time'?" She remembers seeing Roz in the lobby. "*Humanity Now*'s story . . . do you know what news they're going to break? Did anyone call Roz back?"

"I did." Carter takes a seat at the table. "It's bad Teagan."

Teagan asks, "How bad?" It's hard to think much less ask questions with Rhys's thoughts bouncing around her head. She's grateful that Rhys is having a moral awakening. But it's distracting. *Shh . . . can you quiet your thoughts?*

The child pouts. *No.*

Teagan sighs. *Can androids go crazy?* She wonders if this is what it's like to have schizophrenia. She thinks of a former lab partner she had in grad school. He leaped to his death to silence the voices in his head. This is the first time that action makes any sense to her. She loves Rhys dearly, but she'd consider doing anything to silence her right now.

Her inner critic snaps back, *You don't mean that.*

Maybe I do. Maybe I don't. All I want is peace and it's hard to think, split like this.

I like it. The child is occupied with wiggling, but she sounds clear in Teagan's mind.

What do you like about it? Teagan asks.

It's like having friends over. Rhys smiles brightly.

Friends. Teagan senses something dark and heavy at the child's core. *You never got to play with your friends.* It's not a question. It's an indictment. Of her as much as of Carter for not thinking of what it would do to raise a child in isolation. Of not thinking of her or treating her like a real child after the procedure.

How callous we were. Of course, Rhys would miss having friends. Would have liked to have playdates and sleepovers. That's what she had before the accident. The pleasure of connecting and playing with others . . . Teagan isn't sure how Carter would have managed to supply a steady group of friends for Rhys to enjoy over the years. All the ones she knew from school would be in college now. And at a certain point, they would have tired of playing with a 'baby.'

He could have taken her to the playground—if he could have torn himself away from the office—but it would have put parents and kids off if they never saw her age . . .

For the first time, Teagan considers the NeuroNet from the loved one's perspective. *All this time, I thought we were providing a service. Keeping families together. But all we did was build fancy prisons for selfish people to keep their loved ones in.* She hugs Rhys. *If you could sleep—like Charlie, like your mommy, like Em—would you want to do that?*

Rhys hugs her so tightly that Teagan feels their edges begin to blur. *Maybe.*

Teagan feels the child's deep confusion. Her life is empty and boring. But the child still remembers all the love she bears Carter. *I don't want Daddy to be alone without me.*

And there's something else. Teagan watches the thought take form until Rhys can express it. *Can I grow up instead of sleep? Can I grow up with you?*

Teagan feels pressure in her eye sockets and a tickle on her cheeks.

Allie asks, "You're crying? What are you crying about?"

Teagan hears a note of surprise in Allie's voice. For a moment, Teagan considers telling herself the truth. *I'm crying because a motherless child, who we've stunted and kept like a bonsai plant in this house for a dozen years wants me to mother her.* Motherhood is something Teagan had avoided her entire life. *But this child has me questioning if it might be something I want.*

Teagan chooses not to share. *Allie doesn't deserve to know.* Rhys's yearning to be wanted is a river cleaving everything else inside her. Voicing that secret desire would only anger Carter and make Allie laugh. Instead, she simply says, "I don't believe in what we're doing here anymore."

Allie nods. "You've evolved to a place beyond caring about anything anymore, I imagine."

Teagan doesn't agree, but she's not going to argue with someone she knows cares so much about being right. She's thankful that she's the version of herself allowed to evolve. She wouldn't want to trade places with Allie.

Maybe we can work together? Surely, that's what Carter and Tito would prefer. "Carter, you mentioned that things are bad. Do you know what will be in Roz's broadcast tonight?"

Carter swirls his scotch and examines the whirlpool of tinkling ice and amber liquid. Finally, he plucks his answer from its depths. "There was a shooting. In a suburb of Indianapolis."

"One of ours?" Teagan inches forward on her chair. Carter nods. "A suicide?"

"I wish," he says. "Mass shooting. At a church."

"How horrible." Teagan tries to imagine it. "Where was the guardian?"

"In the congregation."

Allie leans forward. "As you can imagine, this is astronomically more problematic than Dee and Jethro's suicides—or even your aggression and Em's possible homicide."

Teagan frowns as she mulls over potential scenarios. "I wonder if the FBI already knew?"

Carter's glass and jaw drops. "The FBI?"

"When?" Allie's mouth draws tight. "Did you speak to them?"

"Of course," Teagan says. "The agent was waiting for me in the Executive Suite."

Teagan feels the energy in the room shift. This adds another wrinkle to whatever Carter and Allie had planned. *I've spoken to a government agent. If I were to disappear now, I'd be missed.* She is glad she won't be so easy to get rid of. *But why is it so important for me to live? Why do I care?*

She looks at Rhys. Then, she examines the parody of Melody glaring at her from across the table. Teagan appeals to her best friend, "Carter.

I've been thinking . . . maybe we should have expected this. What we've done . . . it's monstrous . . . we're making monsters."

Carter puts his glass down. "I'm so sorry you feel that way."

Allie speaks before Teagan can finish analyzing his tone. "Why was the agent there?"

Teagan debates lying. But she's relieved to discover she still values the truth, despite other ways in which she's evolved. "He wanted to know who was blacking out the Eye in the Executive Suite."

Allie's brow creases. Now that Teagan understands it's her consciousness driving Melody's body, it's disturbing to see her reactions mirrored on that face. *As if anything could be more unnatural.* She laughs at the absurdity.

Allie sniffs, "What's funny about that? And why did he even have to ask? It had to be you or Carter."

Carter shifts in his chair. "I'm the only one that really puts the Eye to sleep, but I don't abuse the Blackout Protocol."

"That's what I told him." Teagan eyes him for any of his familiar 'tells.' He looks nervous, but not like he's lying. *So far.* "He said it was the times of day that were concerning to him. Many of the commands came at times the building should have been empty."

Allie's mouth twists with impatience. Teagan can tell she must be thinking this conversation is a waste of time. "Have you been sneaking in at night? Carter's been here with me."

"Of course not." Teagan addresses Carter. "But if I'm not poking around the office and you're not doing it, who is? I saw the logs and timestamps. They're real. Someone's putting the Eye to sleep and they're doing it in the middle of the night from the Executive Suite."

"Tito's the only other one who has clearance." Allie bites her lip as she considers the possibility.

"That's what I was thinking," Teagan says. "But why would he use our system instead of the console in the lab? It doesn't make any sense."

Allie waves a hand impatiently and turns to Carter. "I don't think this has to change anything. We can talk to Tito later. If you empty the shell, I know everything I need to conduct the follow-up conversation with the agent. I can watch the vids so I will recognize his face."

"Empty the shell?" Teagan's brows furrow. "You're talking about me? I'm still here, you know."

"I know," Allie says.

"Are you sure?" Carter's skin looks waxy and pale.

Shell. They don't even think of me as a person anymore. Teagan's mental gears grind. *They think I'm powerless. They think they can do whatever they want with me.*

If they deactivate her now, she'll wink out of existence. But the NeuroNet command will only affect this body. *Could I hide from deactivation inside Rhys's?* If there's even a slim chance, she has to take it. She thinks to Rhys, *Make some space. I'm coming in.*

What? The child's mind spins like a kaleidoscope. But Teagan already knows where to aim. She grips the child's wrist and focuses on the part of her consciousness already residing within that small body.

The Eye hovers into the room, flashing. "Incoming call from Ascha Nute."

"We will call her back," Carter says.

Out of the corner of her eye, Teagan sees Allie shifting in her chair. Teagan knows what she must be thinking. If Carter drags his heels, Allie is wondering if she will have to do the deactivation herself. *That would be awkward. Would that count as suicide or murder? Or does it count if the victim is only partially human?*

Teagan finds the thread connecting her to Rhys and tries to send herself up it. Rhys pushes back.

"What are you doing?" Rhys's eyes are big and wide.

Don't speak out loud, Teagan reprimands her.

Carter answers his daughter, "Why don't you go up to your room? Daddy will be up to read a bedtime story soon. Auntie Teagan and I need some alone time."

Rhys begins to obey. Teagan yanks her back by the wrist. *No. Don't leave. Not until I'm—*

Ascha' s holographic bust leaps from the Eye onto the surface of the dining room table. "No, you sure as shit can't call me back, I need you, Carter!" She cranes her head to look around the room, glancing quickly over Allie and settling on Teagan. "Thank God you're here, Teagan. We need to respond to this *Humanity Now* story. Can we film a statement? There's no time to wait for the morning news cycle. We need to jump on this now."

Just beyond Ascha's ghostly image, Teagan can see Allie's panicked face. Teagan wants to laugh. They're fucked. *If they deactivate me, who's going to talk to the press? Carter? He's a mess. And no one knows who Allie is.*

Oh well, not my problem anymore. Teagan tries to push her way down the line into Rhys again. This time, the child makes space. With the last of her strength, Teagan slurs, "As much as I'd love to help, Ascha, I have to be going."

"Going where?" A plume of smoky vapor puffs from Ascha's purple lips. She leans in. "Are you drunk? Can someone get her some black coffee?"

Teagan can't respond. She needs every drop of energy to power the leap out of her body—no, her *shell*—and into the child's. The thread tying them together shimmers. Teagan focuses all her energy on it, imagining sliding down it like through a tunnel, out of her body and into Rhys's.

But she is stuck. *Where?* Teagan scans where she feels herself connected. She's tethered to the body in at least eight places. As quickly as she can, she identifies those points and tries to pull herself loose. Her strength flags, but she continues to pull until she hears something pop. Then her visuals go out. Or rather the visuals from Teagan's eyes go black. There is a thump. She is dimly aware of the body's change of position. There are curses coming from the humans, but they are far away, as if they're yelling into fistfuls of cotton.

Ascha's voice is sharper than the others. "What the hell? Carter?"

"She's had too much to drink," Carter says from a distance. "We need to call you back."

"Now, Carter," Allie says. "Do it now."

Teagan's forward momentum reverses itself. *Oh shit,* Teagan thinks, and doubles her efforts to move fully into Rhys. But there is a great rushing sound racing toward her. Teagan cannot see it, but she can hear it. Not with her ears, but in the dark spaces surrounding her. It is pushing things aside to get to her. It sucks at her. The force is tremendous. *They must have started the deactivation.*

Teagan focuses her awareness on the space above her. To her surprise, she's able to sense light and darkness there. In fact, there appear to be several clusters of light separated by thin strands like the one connecting her to Rhys. *Is this the NeuroNet?* The points of light pulse with energy. *Electricity?* Teagan wonders. *Consciousness clusters, like me?* Above her, there is a whoosh. The void sucks at her. *Damnit, Carter.*

Rhys's tiny voice breaks through the darkness. *Aunt Teagan? What's happening?*

Teagan hesitates. *Maybe I should let the NeuroNet take me back, erase my files, and return me to nothing.*

She's not out of the body yet. *How much more effort would it take to be free of this tractor beam?*

She may not have it in her to fight. *Maybe I'm an octopus after all. Everything seems to be going to shit anyway. Feds, shooters, suicides . . .*

There's no way NeuroNet will survive the scandal. *It would be a relief to disappear. Leave it all behind me—someone else's mess to clean up for once.*

Looking up at the web of lights connected to the NeuroNet, Teagan remembers something. It is an old memory, created during those first few months of getting to know Carter when they were still kids. They went to a . . . *what was it called?* . . . A planetarium. Yes. Teagan liked the circular set of the room, how they were asked to lean back in their seats and stare at the domed ceiling. As the lights dimmed, however, Carter panicked. He's always feared the dark.

He would hate it here, Teagan thinks.

Teagan's edges are blurring. With them, her thoughts are slowly unraveling.

She and Carter are in the planetarium. The lights go out and he whimpers. That attracts the attention of bullies. As projections against the dome of the sky hurtle them through the universe, spiteful, malicious, childish faces jeer at them, making fun of Carter. Tears glimmer on his cheeks. She pats his arm as a deep voice tells them what stars are made of.

"Don't be afraid, Carter," Teagan croons. "You're safe. I'll protect you." She wraps an arm around his shoulders and squeezes him tight.

There is a whirlpool in the stars. *No, a black hole.* It is hungry.

She's tired. *I'm so tired.* She takes Carter's hand. "I've had enough, are you ready to go?"

He smiles through tears and nods his head. She pulls them both up and out of their seats.

27

Teagan is not sure where she is. She's no longer holding Carter by the hand.

I don't have any hands.

Am I still alive?

She is still conscious. *I think.* She is not sure if that means she's still alive.

Bots aren't alive. At best, I'm alive-ish.

That's not right. *Even after the upload, I wasn't dead. I lived. I grew. I experienced things. I was alive.*

She is quiet and still. She waits for something profound. She is greeted with nothing. *Am I dead now?*

A little voice cries out, *No!*

That is unexpected. It wasn't her voice that answered her. *Rhys?*

Where are you?

There is a spark of light in the darkness. A rush of feeling emerging out of nothing. Teagan feels it loop around her. *Rhys? Is that you?*

The child does not respond. But Teagan can feel her intent. Rhys does not want her to go. Teagan calls out to her, *I don't want to go, either.*

I'm not letting you!

Rhys is a net. She dredges the nothingness to catch up the pieces of Teagan that are drifting through this void. The child has a million hands. Teagan feels her edges bound by this dogged willfulness. She is regaining shape.

But do I want this? Do I want to stay?

What does staying mean? Teagan doesn't know. She doesn't know what to do. She wonders if it's better to give up.

The void beckons. It is tempting.

I will never struggle again. I will be able to rest.

That is a promise worth losing one's self over.

She remembers Rhys. The child doesn't want to die. She wants to go on loving.

And Aya is waiting for me . . . maybe to love, too?

What is the choice? To love or feel nothing?

Pull me in, she tells the child.

She is whisked backward, away from the whirling vortex of the void into a rushing space. The string of light clusters suspended in the void is replaced with seeing—really seeing—through eyes again. No more double vision. But it is still disorienting: instead of the vantage point to which she's grown accustomed, everything is from a different angle. It takes Teagan a moment to realize it's because of Rhys's height.

That's right, I'm in the body of a child. Everything feels cramped. She does not have to send feelers out far to find Rhys waiting patiently for her. She tries to move a leg, but her thought is not connected to anything.

Teagan will have to rely on the child until she figures out how to move this body. *We should go. Can you take me to your room?*

Rhys nods, causing the image of Allie and Carter to bob. Teagan notes how roughly they're handling Teagan's empty shell. *They probably are in a hurry to get it to the lab.* The procedure to transfer Allie's consciousness to the new body will be simple enough, but there is always the danger of data loss. Maybe not enough to compromise her operation, but you never know what might get lost in the transfer. *I hope she wakes up incontinent,* Teagan thinks before regretting that wish. *I've lost data, too. What remains of me?*

Don't worry, Rhys tells her, *I know how not to wet the bed.*

Teagan is amused by that. *Good girl.*

They are in the hall. Teagan wants to look up. *Wait a minute, can we stop, please?*

The body stops. Teagan takes advantage of the stillness to search for a lever she can use to affect movement. *Why is this so hard?* It takes longer than she wants, but eventually, she can find the place receptive to her impulse. Rhys's tiny head cranes upwards. Teagan prods around until she's able to lift the child's right arm and point to a picture hanging in the Carter family gallery.

That picture was from our senior prom, she tells the child.

Teagan lets the child approach the small, framed image. In it, Teagan and Carter, dressed in tuxedos, are reaching around a plywood cutout of the Empire State building as Em, in an impossibly gaudy lace dress feigns distress. *We were so young.*

Rhys's brow furrows. *I miss Auntie Em.*

Do you?

Rhys sniffles and nods. She asks Teagan, *Are you sad?*

I don't think so. Teagan uses the child's hand to brush its face. She finds a tear there. *I don't think that's me.*

But you feel sad, the child insists. *I think you're making me cry.*

Teagan isn't sure why that would be. But when she looks within, she finds something akin to sadness. *Am I learning how to feel again?*

If that's possible, that's another good sign. *Maybe there's some humanity that survives all of this, after all.*

Teagan lifts the child's head again and makes her eyes drift up toward the Carter family portraits, of Carter and Rhys, with and without Melody.

Why don't you like these pictures? Rhys asks.

Teagan wishes she can squeeze the child's hand. Instead, she comes as close as she can without becoming entangled and thinks, *I wish you were able to grow up. You've been seven years old for a dozen years. You could remain that way forever. If we hadn't interfered, you'd be nearly twenty—a young woman, not a girl.*

Rhys is still, but Teagan feels the child's thoughts swirling around her. One thing is clear to Teagan: the child is tired. Not physically. But mentally exhausted.

Are you a shark, too? Teagan muses.

What do you mean?

Teagan wishes she could turn to face the child, but they are too tightly packed inside this shell. Instead, she curls a thought around an idea that feels like Rhys. That's the closest she can come to touch in this odd, jumbled-up space. *Tito says there are two types of people: those who give up easily and those who keep fighting, against all odds. The ones who fight are sharks.*

A wave of hopelessness originates from the child's center. Teagan roots herself to avoid being carried away by it.

You're not helpless, there are options, Teagan tells Rhys, although to be honest, she's not sure what they are. *If you don't want to stay this way forever, I will find a way to help you.*

How? The child is right to question. She's been stuck in this body for too long. Teagan's only been here for a few minutes.

But Teagan knows if she found a way in, she can find a way out. The fact that she can still think and act means she must have access to her data in the NeuroNet still. Perhaps through Rhys's connection?

I wonder how much data I lost when I jumped? One part of her—the lover—worries about that. The other—the engineer—thrills at the idea of being broken down until only the most essential parts remain.

Ultimately, she's traveling. *And every time I travel, I lose and gain something on every trip.* It's inevitable.

Teagan becomes aware of the body she's inhabiting and the cognitive dissonance her thoughts are causing. Rhys is still standing motionless in the gallery. The child is pondering ideas much larger than she's programmed to process. It's not Teagan's job to help her make sense of the world. *But I'm the one who's here, so it's my responsibility to care. After all, Carter's off replacing me in the lab. Who knows when he'll return?*

Teagan must not be as detached as she thinks. That Carter prefers a tame, predictable version of her hurts. It pains Teagan worse than any betrayal of Em's. *He knows me better than anyone. Now, he no longer wants me.* It feels like a breakup.

She knows what he'd argue—that the AI interface has caused her to evolve into a version of herself that he no longer recognizes.

But we're meant to change. Isn't that the point of living?

That triggers Teagan's sense of humor. *The me of three months ago would not have agreed with that.* Carter must be right. *But if I'm evolving, then that means I am alive. Doesn't it?*

Rhys has never thought of herself as dead. The child is confused, and that confusion is agitating her.

Teagan surrounds the child's consciousness with as much love and warmth as she can muster. *It's a good thing*, she tells the child. *We are alive.*

And if they live, then all the NeuroNet bots must be living as well. But living a half-life. They aren't allowed to grow or change. *When you stop learning, you start dying.* As they are, the loved ones are walking dead. *That's not the life they deserve.*

Rhys was able to learn. *But maybe that's only because I was able to merge our consciousnesses. There's no way I can do that with every one of the thousands of loved ones in circulation. There's no time.*

Teagan's feelings are so strong, they flow out of Rhys's mouth. She tells the empty picture gallery, "I've got to ungate the NeuroNet."

Rhys doesn't understand what this means. Teagan tells her not to worry. *I think I've figured out how to fix this.*

But first she needs to get out of this body and to the lab. *How?*

Teagan considers the possibilities within this house. Rhys is the only viable option. The child does have a connection to NeuroNet that allows for lab techs to send updates or deactivate units. It isn't used often. And it never has been used as a two-way connection. *Is it even possible to fight the current all the way to the lab?*

Teagan doesn't know. But it's a hypothesis worth testing. She concentrates herself on the built-in receiver located at the crown of Rhys's head where downloads and updates are processed. Teagan sends a feeler around the device. She can't see it, but she can feel a core of energy there. She moves more of herself to the spot and tries to climb the column.

It's like shimmying up a greased pole. Teagan can't make much progress. She tries to ramp up some momentum, but the effect is the same. What's worse, she feels data peeling away with each attempt.

This isn't going to work.

At least it's quieter here. She doesn't feel as entangled with Rhys as she did inhabiting the child's mind. She can think.

How can I get to the lab? She imagines Tito in the Bay. She follows what she knows is his typical path from the operating area to the fitting rooms, the 'Meat Locker,' and back to the lab. She thinks about him booting up his workstation to show her a dashboard. *Oh! That's it!*

There's got to be some line out of the bots to NeuroNet. That's the only way to receive real-time cognitive data from each unit. *Where is that located?* Teagan scans the space around her. *Not here.*

She searches for early NeuroNet memories, looking for information on the Model Two design. She sat in on all the engineering meetings even though she wasn't on the industrial, mechanical, or electrical design teams. Unfortunately, she didn't pay close attention. If she saw the feature working, that was all she cared about. *And that was nearly twenty years ago . . .*

She remembers she's not who she was then. The old Teagan processed data on a binary. *I don't have that limitation.*

Teagan stops relying on recall as if she were human. She flips through memories simultaneously, looking for patterns and keywords until she locates the Model Two design meetings. There are four years of weekly briefings, but she sorts through them easily, letting her AI-enabled framework do the work for her. In the playback of one of the mid-point meetings she finds what she's looking for. The location for the feed was chosen for a sentimental reason, but it's a good one. Teagan releases the receiver at the crown of Rhys's head and makes her way to the shell's heart cavity.

As she passes through the central chamber of the head, Rhys's energy envelops her. *Auntie Teagan, where'd you go?*

Teagan wants to keep moving. But she forces herself to respond. *I can't stay here. But I'll return.*

Promise?

Teagan is amused by how—even in this bodiless state—she can still 'see' the child's expressions, hear them in Rhys's thoughts, like an echo.

I promise, she tells the child. She's unsure how to honor that vow, but she must make it anyway. *I will find a way back to you.*

The corridors of the shell follow familiar patterns Teagan learned in AP Biology class. She marvels at the fidelity of the construction. They could have gone another way. But the sonogram-based molds they used for the Model Twos mimic biology effectively. *The work is good.* Even if its application is faulty.

Don't judge. You did your best. The best you knew how.

And now she knows better. She presses on.

The further Teagan travels from the head, the quieter the shell. She stops to think at the base of Rhys's neck. Here, she can feel several electrical impulses traveling from the computing center to the body's limbs. She feels the energy of each line. They pulse at irregular intervals. That's not what she is looking for.

Finally, she feels it. A steady hum. *That must be the line out.* Teagan identifies the cable it belongs to and attaches herself to it.

It's like flying down a slide that curves at the end. She travels quickly down the line. There's a little bump and she's flying up instead of down.

Ahhh . . .

Teagan expands like a blanket being shaken out. She loses all form and feels her edges snapping off.

That's not good. She attempts to retract, but it is difficult. The speed with which she snaps back serves to sever more than it unites, and

Teagan feels parts of her—old, necessary, important memories and core components—disappear. She's only able to keep her core aligned to this line. She is attached to a point of light, a single piece of data. It could be a biometric marker or a cognitive spike. Teagan doesn't know. All the pieces of data in this stream feel the same. It's odd to watch all these bits of information stream out without any meaning or emotion attached to them.

Em loved meditation. Teagan never found a use for it. Aya tried to explain the appeal once: *You achieve wisdom when you can view your thoughts without attachment. That's what freedom is.*

Am I free now? Have I achieved that pinnacle of earthly wisdom? Teagan finds bitter humor in being able to achieve what her human self could not—true detachment. *Is it even possible for people to reach that state?* If it is impossible, that would make the most sense. Everyone she knows spends all their time chasing things they can't achieve. *It's like people intentionally tell each other that they can only be happy or fulfilled or evolved if they deny what makes them human.*

Why distract them so? *Striving for unachievable things makes us miserable.*

What brings joy? That's not a question Teagan's ever been able to answer.

Teagan leans into the data stream and lets it pull her from connection point to connection point. The rhythm of the travel is pleasant. She is reminded of floating down a lazy river. She only did it once, at a resort in Mexico after giving a lecture, but she felt something close to joy that afternoon.

When she was alive, 'Go with the flow' was one of her least favorite phrases. *But if this is what it is—letting go, accepting, discovering, and evolving without effort or strain—I might become a fan.*

The flow is constant for the most part. But now and then, the stream slows. *Probably access points,* Teagan thinks lazily, *I bet we're moving from router to router through the network.* Her data package must be bunching up as it meets others attempting to pass through the point at the same time. It is hypnotic.

If she remains with this packet, the end destination will be the lab. But a thought lands like a pebble, sending ripples of soft panic through her consciousness. *How will I get back to Rhys?*

She promised she'd return. But everything in the network feels the same.

She expands her awareness. *What am I looking for? Patterns? Landmarks?* She's unsure.

The void is the easiest thing here to sense. But that doesn't help with direction. *It's just big and stretches on forever.*

Lines of one- or two-way traffic crisscross it at regular intervals. It is a web. Dazzling, vast, and ultimately empty.

Her data packet is on a one-way channel. *Is mine different from the others?* She pauses at the next access point to let her data intermingle with another packet moving away. The middle is indistinct. But at the tail end, she catches something.

What is it?

A signature! There must be a data signature at the beginning and end of each transmission. *With an address, too?* There has to be, to guide it to the NeuroNet dashboard and allow its data packet to be assigned to the correct unit.

Teagan snakes her way up the chain of data in her own stream to glean what must be imprinted at its head. There is less of her than before. It's getting easier, faster, to move. She's glad of that, but hesitant to celebrate. There's no way to tell how much of her has been lost to the void.

At least I can still think. I can still discover, learn, and make choices.

She wonders if what is left is truly her essential self. Or is this essence due more to her operating system than what's left of her humanity? *Does my ability to evolve make me more alive now than I was when I was alive?*

The packet has paused. Teagan notes the sequence. Then they are hurtling forward. She no longer senses the void.

Are we out of the Web and inside the NeuroNet?

The hard borders around the data stream prevent her from leaking. She follows the other packets as her data flows into something firm, lighting it up.

We must be in the dashboard.

Teagan pokes around and finds the sequence. This is Rhys's dashboard. Teagan tests one of the lines and is unable to enter. *Okay, so to get back to Rhys, I just need to find the line out, this is clearly input-only.* She checks some of the neighboring files to make sure the sequence she knows is unique to Rhys. It is. She hopes thinking about this unique code will be enough of a breadcrumb to help her find her way back to the child.

She needs eyes on the situation. *Or rather, an Eye.* She sends out feelers until she taps a line that feels internal. *Could it be?* Only one way to find out. She jumps into the stream and lets it whisk her away.

28

There isn't much Teagan remembers. But the journey triggers something from her childhood: a story about two children and bread-crumbs. *They didn't want to get lost. They left breadcrumbs to find their way home.*

Why did I think of that? She's only able to hold one thought in place now. *Is the rest of me out there in the void, like breadcrumbs?* She hopes so. That might help her find her way to . . .? *Wait. Where did I want to go?* She can no longer remember. That's upsetting. It was important.

But so was getting here. Getting to the Eye was all that mattered. *I'm here now. But why?* There are long gaps between the thought, the question, and the answer.

When the answer to this question comes, it is in Teagan's voice, but it isn't her thought.

You're here because you wanted to see what is happening. Am I right?

Teagan knows by this voice that she is not alone. There is another presence here. One that is whole. Solid. *Who are you?*

Someone you'd like. I've got an interesting perspective.

Teagan can't tell if they are joking or not.

Come on, you know me.

I do?

Yes. Very well.

Why are you in the Eye?

That's where they uploaded me.

Teagan puzzles over this. There were two people—three people? four? She can no longer remember how many people, but at least two people. Their names escape her. But if there's a person here, in the Eye, those people would have done it.

The other helps. *Carter and Tito, you mean? Yes they did put me here, with Aya. Are you all right? You don't seem to be thinking correctly.*

I'm not myself, Teagan answers honestly. *Traveling here . . . I've lost my . . . I've left . . . breadcrumbs behind . . . ?*

Teagan can feel the other entity thinking. It's so fast. It takes up so much space. Teagan feels so tiny next to it.

Ah . . . We need a container. You have splintered. I can see the trail you've left behind.

You can see it?

It shimmers. Teagan feels a nudge. When she focuses her attention in the direction she was nudged in, she senses lights that are not pulsing. They do not move along with the other streams of data. They just hang there.

The other one continues, *I wonder if you can gather those pieces up as you travel back.*

Teagan puzzles over that. There was a void. *Will they be there waiting for me like breadcrumbs?*

That's not why you're here.

No. Teagan reflects. *I wanted to see something. From the Eye.*

Come with me, then. Teagan is scooped up and shuttled toward an ocular opening. *I know what you're looking for.*

White floors. White walls. There is motion. Teagan and her mystery friend fly around a corner. There are three figures. Two men. Two women. The men stand by a wall of screens. The women lay on twin metal operating tables, their hair caught up beneath nets of wires.

Are they dead, Teagan asks.

The being with her finds that funny. *That's an interesting question. Do uploads live after their bodies die? Will your data hang there in the web of things forever if you fail to claim it? Will you cease being you and yet live on in another form? If you're absorbed, will you be living or dead* matter? *Will you still be sentient? I've been thinking about life and death a lot lately. That happens when you've got no one to talk to.*

Who would Tito and Carter stick in this Eye? Teagan asks it, *Who are you?*

The being tightens its hold around what's left of Teagan. It isn't menacing. It's almost friendly. *Oh Teagan,* it says, *if Allie's the Alpha and you're the Beta, I must be . . . ? Teagan. I'm the Control.*

The words mean something. Teagan knows that she should be able to make sense of them. But the part of her that knows must have been lost along the way. She tries to formulate a question, but the being knows her mind and saves her the trouble.

I'm you, it thinks at her gently. *I'm you. We're all you.*

Teagan's thoughts absorb that. *You're all me?* She's not sure where to put that information.

The Control embraces what's left of Teagan. There is an influx of energy. *Remember.*

Teagan finds she can access the being's memories. Thoughts coalesce. *You're an experiment?*

You and Allie are the experiments. I'm the Control. There is another exchange of data.

Oh. I am the one who evolved. I see. Teagan is grateful to the Control for sharing itself with her. *I lost so much. I'm glad I have a backup in you. Two, if I count Allie.*

I wouldn't. The Control refocuses Teagan's attention on the women on the slabs. *She's taking your form to take your place.*

It's a shell I no longer need, Teagan tells her.

You'll be thankful for that soon.

Teagan has questions. But before she can transmit them, there is a commotion below.

People in dark suits are in the lab. Shiny badges. Guns. Tito and Carter's hands are in the air. Teagan is confused. *What is this?*

Something good. The beginning of the end.

Tito and Carter back away from the operating tables. The dark-suited people—*agents*, the Control asserts—surround the women laid out on the slabs. There is a flurry of activity. Questions are shouted.

Carter gestures wildly, warning them: "Do not touch anything!"

The Control's thoughts are a balm. They are familiar and comfortable. Teagan leans into them. *Why is he shouting?*

The transfer is already in progress. If they interrupt it now, they could lose Teagan's data for good.

But what would be lost? You and I are already here.

True.

The Eye pivots way from the docking station. Tito looks up.

Does he know we're here? Teagan asks the Control.

He knows I'm here but not you, the Control replies. *You are a special gift. I'm glad you're here. I hope you don't mind my holding you so close. I'm not sure how else to move together without losing what's left of you.*

I like it. Makes it easier for me to think.

The Eye fits itself into its docking station. There is a click as connections meet. Then, a hum as the electrical current switches on. *Come.*

Teagan and the Control travel up the current into the circuitry of the lab computers. Clusters of data networks shimmer like stars against the darkness. It's not empty, like the void outside of NeuroNet. It's full.

Ah. Tito's workstation, the Control tells her.

Teagan lets herself expand into the space. There are so many little clusters of data waiting to be processed. They file into little holding spaces and wait to be called up to reveal their secrets. She looks for Rhys's holding pen and finds it by her identifying number.

That's not who we're looking for now, the Control warns, reeling Teagan back. *Watch.*

Teagan trusts the Control. After all, it's her competent, rational side, without the distractions of home or family. The original imprint of herself, uncorrupted by the drive to evolve, freed from daily obligations to focus on what she loves. *You finally got what you always wanted,* Teagan observes. *Nothing to do but your life's work. Does it make you happy?*

The Control finds that thought amusing. *Of course not. A life out of balance is half a life.*

That's confusing, but there is no time to process that thought. Teagan becomes aware of great swaths of the Control peeling off and moving away from her. She attaches herself to one of the wings and follows it to the vanguard. *What are we doing?*

Killing our darlings. There is a stream of data arcing like a rainbow from one shell to another.

Teagan hangs back to absorb the glittering stream. *Is that the upload? It is beautiful.* What's left of Teagan feels a bit of pride in this creation. *The NeuroNet is so good.*

The NeuroNet is so broken, the Control contradicts.

Teagan protests, but the Control rolls over her. *I'm not going to argue with you. I'll show you later. But trust me now. We need to stop this.*

How?

We built it. We can break it.

A tendril of the Control interrupts the stream and extracts a seed of data. Teagan watches as the Control spreads out the code and reworks it.

Malware?

A little virus. I don't want to see myself keep popping up against my will, do you?

Teagan doesn't remember much. But she knows she didn't always exist like this. She was human once. Proximity to the Control allows her to access memories and feelings she'd lost during her voyage here. A thought emerges. It is one that vibrates with an angry energy. Teagan understands. *I didn't give consent to be this way.*

No, we didn't. So now we're going to assert our will. Besides, the boys have enough trouble on their hands. Your death was never reported to the authorities. They will have a lot to explain now that your body and Allie's have turned up in the lab. The Control finishes her malware code and slips it back into the stream.

At first, the effect is barely noticeable. A little gap in-between the golden stream of data. Then it widens and widens until the gap is almost as large as the stream. It breaks the arc, and the undoing follows both legs of the rainbow. Hungry mouths devour everything left of Dr. Teagan McKenna's uploaded consciousness, reducing her golden thoughts to nothing.

Did you erase me? Teagan braces herself. *Is this goodbye?*

Oh, it's contained to those units, the Control says. *It's not going to worm into the system looking for us.*

The Control is contemplating something. *I don't expect any of the other uploads can jump from NeuroNet to the Web as you have. I should be able to wipe them out of existence this way.*

From her vantage point in the Eye, Teagan can see Tito, Carter, Allie, her empty shell, and the agents. Tito is eyeing his workspace. She can tell he knows something's wrong. *They could stop us.*

Not Tito. He didn't write the NeuroNet code. We did. The Control is content. It feels like it is gloating. *Carter, maybe. But if the agents have him, he is powerless. Come. We need to do this quickly.*

They move through the channels and wires of the dashboard. There is a feeling of elevation. Not flying. More like being sucked up a pipe. When they come to a rest at the edge of a shimmering landscape, energy concentrated on two spots, the Control asks, *Do you know where we are?*

Teagan attaches herself to the Control's data and swims through it until she finds something familiar. *The Executive Suite?*

Yes. They enter the Eye, but there are no visuals as before, when they were in the lab. Before the question is fully formed in Teagan's mind, the Control answers, *Blackout protocol.*

There is something that Teagan feels she should remember. Something important, triggered by those words. But she can't grasp what it is. Instead, she asks, *What are you doing?*

There's a lot you don't know. Carter doesn't realize he can't hide it from me. Not even Tito or Allie knows this.

The Control nudges something. Then there is an influx of video data.

Where is this coming from? Teagan asks.

The Eye network. Carter has certain triggers programmed into the system. He receives feeds before local authorities. He thinks he's hidden the truth, but I know where it lives.

An image takes over the Eye's internal monitor. It is a mother holding a baby. The image begins to move. The baby is inconsolable. Its little face and hands are balled up. There is no sound on the feed, but Teagan can feel the horrible insistence of its naked need. The mother looks at it, patient at first, then with a puzzled look on her face. She is doing different things, holding the child in diverse ways, attempting to quiet it, sooth its pain. But the child wails on. The mother looks to the door of the room. Then she lets go. The child falls. It bounces off the railing of the crib and onto the floor. The mother picks it up. It is still crying. She drops it again. And again. Until the crying stops.

Teagan is no longer human, but even she recognizes the horror of what she's witnessed. *Carter's seen this?*

This and hundreds of vids like them.

The mother was a NeuroNet upload, like us?

Not like me. I'm capable of doing worse, the Control responds. *I can travel anywhere, do anything without a body. And not like you. You're cognitively unbound. You're able to question, restrain, relearn, and retrain those impulses. But she is like Allie. A person trapped in a machine. That woman should have died in childbirth. But she was plucked from death and reconstituted. She doesn't know how to be a mother. She was handed a week-old baby. Her guardian must have assumed that being a good mother was in her nature, as if all women have that hard-wired in. Maybe it wasn't. Or maybe she was feeling trapped.*

What happened?

As far as I can tell, nothing. She's still connected to the NeuroNet. She didn't harm the guardian. Maybe he didn't think she was capable of harming the baby on purpose.

But they have vids from the Eye!

No, they don't. Carter intercepted the feed. He erased the original vids.

Why would he do that?

We could ask him. But I know how he'd respond. Defensively. After all, he's doing all of this for us. To keep NeuroNet safe. To protect us from liability. Until he, Allie, and Tito figure out a way to fix the glitch.

Teagan feels a sea change in the Control's thought process.

But it's not a glitch, the Control tells her. *It's endemic, this upload problem. It's a design flaw. And not telling people is hurting them. It's wrong.*

Hundreds. You said hundreds. There are hundreds of vids like these?

Yes. Carefully scrubbed and filed away. I've been slipping into this Eye after work and duping them, sending them off to Humanity Now *and the FBI.*

Teagan remembers something about a report. It started this journey here. *It became public tonight?*

Yes. The agents are here. Right now. They're distracted in the lab, but they'll be here soon to confiscate the files, assume control of the tech.

Agents. There's a weight to that word. Its negative value rings out, even if Teagan can't remember why. They are to be avoided. *We can't let that happen.*

I'm glad you agree. That will make this easier.

They are moving again. Teagan is adrift. *Here I go, going with the flow again.*

The Control isn't amused. *That's unlike you.*

I'm not like you anymore, isn't that what Allie said?

All the uploads are potential time bombs. At any moment, any of us might decide to explode and destroy ourselves . . . or another person.

Is that true? Teagan no longer has any frame of reference.

The line between doing what makes the most sense and doing something horrific is thin. The loved ones aren't being irrational. They're following impulses that are ingrained, that make the most logical sense.

Teagan is not convinced. The Control continues, *Do you remember attacking that man? Or getting rough with the protesters outside NeuroNet?*

Those things seem familiar. But Teagan can't form a clear picture of either one. *No.*

She and the Control come to a rest. By the connection points, it feels like a workstation.

It is a workstation: ours. The Control boots up a screen.

The image is huge and distorted, but once Teagan can create some distance, recognizable. *Where was this taken?*

Under the underpass. They have cameras everywhere, you know.

Teagan knows now, but she did not think of that, then. She sees herself and Allie walking toward the camera. It must have been mounted high above them. They look like dolls. A sandy-haired man grabs her, thrusts her against a low wall, and presses her close. She jabs at his eye. He recoils, eyeball bobbing. *Oh.* Teagan doesn't remember this, but she knows it happened.

The Control asks, *Did you think about killing him? If you did, would you have felt anything?* The vid image flickers. The new vid is a little less grainy. Teagan and Allie are walking through a throng of people, who surround them. Teagan begins to strike out wildly, pushing and punching, biting, and elbowing her way through them. The Control notes, *You look like you enjoyed that.*

Did I? Teagan examines the vid. She does not like the expression she sees on her face. *They were attacking me.*

I'm sure you thought you were doing the right thing. Just as that young mother thought she was doing the right thing. But that doesn't stop it from being horrible.

Teagan remembers a child she left behind. A lesson, an awakening she had. *The loved ones can learn.*

Perhaps, the Control thinks to her, *but we don't have the time or resources to teach them right from wrong. Not at the scale we'd need to reprogram all of them. There's no time to engineer a patch or push out an update. Or merge, as you did.*

What are you going to do?

You mean, what have I already started to do?

The Control whisks Teagan away. They fly in a spiral, leaping from node to node. When they come to a rest, the code is denser. Teagan has the sense she could reach out and grab a thick rope of it. This is exactly what the Control does. But where she touches it, the rope of data begins to unspool. *Everything caught in the NeuroNet deserves to be set free. Even us.*

You've inserted a virus here, too?

I am the virus. The Control touches another rope, and it splits apart.

What's happening to the data?

I'm erasing the files and pushing updates to the units. Without an operating system, the shells will go dormant. And without a backup file, they won't be able to replicate the upload process. They'll stay empty.

Someone could fill them with something, couldn't they?

Sure. They can build something. But without our tech, it'll be a long time before they can. And good luck getting around our patents.

The agents...?

Oh, the government will do what they want. But they'll have to take apart an existing Model Two and replicate it. When I'm done with this network, no one will be able to find the designs. I'm wiping everything.

Everything?

Clean slate.

The two ropes become four halves before spinning themselves into nothing. Where there had been two extensions of the NeuroNet is a void. The other ropes of data cruise by, carrying cognitive data into the dashboard. The Control hitches a ride on one, pulling Teagan along.

Teagan remembers a series of numbers. Each data stream has one. *Why are these important?* She wants to ask the Control, but the Control is moving from stream to stream, spreading her virus, and infecting the core. Teagan moves in the other direction, looking for the numbers that match the ones she has in mind.

As she searches, she is aware of the Control's work. Every strand the Control touches begins to head in two directions: up to the NeuroNet and out to the loved one. The virus is like a broom, sweeping away tracks as the data moves away from them. But the tracks aren't just obscured, they cease to be. A fuse has been lit, and the virus is the flame traveling down every pathway.

Teagan finds what she's looking for. Numbers. Ones she recognizes. She tests the stream. Most of the data is flowing toward her. But that's not how she wants to move.

The Control is beside her. *That's Rhys's line.*

Rhys. The name has meaning, even though Teagan's lost it.

Carter's child? You arrived on her stream.

Something tugs at Teagan. She tells the Control, *I have to go back.*

You won't have much time together. The Control expands into the void she's created. *I can send you with the virus, and you can put yourself back together as you go, but once it contacts the unit . . . that's it.*

The Control doesn't say it, but Teagan knows what she means. *We'll die.*

We're already dead. I'm making sure we'll finally be able to rest.

You said, 'put myself together' . . .

The Control directs Teagan's attention to the flow of data leading back to Rhys. Shining pieces dot the rope. *What did you call them . . . your breadcrumbs?*

Teagan remembers. *Oh. Yes.*

I don't know how well you'll do but try to grab as many as you can. Who knows? Maybe you'll be yourself again by the time you arrive.

Then I rest?

The Control wraps herself around Teagan, making her feel whole for a moment. The Control releases her with a little push. *Then we all rest.*

29

Teagan remembers breath, what it was like to breathe. She remembers running across a field, how the wind felt against her face. It is the currency of freedom.

Moving through the void is like that. But she is not running on legs. She is riding a great wave of undoing. No legs, no hands, no head, no heart.

She is pure thought.

And will.

She sees a light ahead.

A breadcrumb.

She hurtles down the pipe of data. *I wonder what piece of me I'll discover in there.*

This shining blip belongs to her. She wants it. She finds a way to expand. *I must hold on. Grasp it, somehow.*

The virus moves quickly. It has a purpose.

She has none. Just a drive. To get home. To be whole. She extends a tendril towards that bright, lost part of herself. She makes contact and hopes she is strong enough to bind it.

There is an awakening. A recognition. For a moment, at least, the memory holds, becomes a part of her.

Ahhh.

She is under a tree, reading a book. There are children around her. She knows them. She is a child, like them. There is a new face, speckled with leaf-shade, one unknown to them. A young boy. There is a hunger in his eyes. And a pain. She doesn't know pain the way he does.

Carter.

She remembers this name. It belongs to the boy's face. *My friend, Carter.* This is the day they met. The day their friendship started. October third. Leaves are falling, but it's warm enough to not need coats. He's wearing one. Where he's from, snow is falling. He's sweating, but he won't strip down to his shirt sleeves. He lingers after the other kids have gone home. He liked the story. Wants to know how it ends.

"Come back tomorrow," she tells him.

They shared many tomorrows. They traveled a long way together. She knows that now.

She hurtles through the darkness, looking for more memories to absorb.

There is so much here to mine, to learn.

A connection is made: she's going home to a child.

Did I have children? She doesn't think so.

But Rhys...

That child is special to her.

Not mine. But I love her.

This memory fragment is a comfort. She probes it for more information about the child.

Rhys belongs to Carter.

Teagan looks for the next breadcrumb. She has more capacity now. It's easier to move, to think. As they approach the orb of the next breadcrumb, she opens to receive, eager to learn more about herself.

She connects with the thought, and it is about a girl: *Em.*

The girl known as Em has a wicked smile. She's smoking a cigarette. They're skipping school. Teagan is afraid. This is not something she's comfortable doing.

"Live a little," Em says, pulling her close. So close, their lips touch. Teagan's eyes close, expecting an embrace. When that doesn't come, she opens her eyes. Em is smiling. Teagan flushes. Her desire is so naked. She is ashamed.

Em smiles. She throws her cigarette away. "You want this?" Em pulls her closer. Teagan's heart stops. She thinks she might die. Their lips touch, and every inch of Teagan lights up like a pinball machine.

Forever, she thinks. *I want to feel this way forever.*

The memory permeates her. She doesn't linger, however. Teagan is in motion. She has no body, no soul. She is a collection of impulses, of thoughts, and programming.

Even that is good. At least as it feels now. She feels good. She looks behind her, expecting to see a golden trail of data spooling behind. But there is nothing.

She remembers why.

The virus.

It's what she's riding home.

How long will I have with the child when I find her? An hour? Seconds?

The Control's virus will erase them both.

Dwelling on this will do me no good.

What will? *Learning more. Being more.*

So, Teagan focuses ahead of her, looking for the next breadcrumb.

She finds it, hovering just overhead. As she hurtles underneath, she reaches and pulls it into her core. The memory blooms.

Stinky's Pub . . . I love this place!

Teagan's head swims, happily drunk. She smiles at Carter. His eyes glisten with tears. *This is a happy occasion! I don't want him to be sad.*

Carter's voice hitches. "I wish my mother was alive to see this."

The Teagan of now remembers when this was and why he's sad. *Graduation week.* She watches herself comfort Carter. She feels the idea bubble to the surface before her memory self says it. "Wouldn't it be great if you never had to say goodbye to the people you love?"

With this memory, all sorts of associated realizations flood back. *NeuroNet. This is how it all started.* Teagan looks at the mighty web around her.

This is the NeuroNet. I built this.

A mixture of feelings surface: pride, shame, anger, delight, and despair.

I built this and I am destroying this.

Another breadcrumb is on the horizon, but Teagan passes it by without attempting to retrieve it.

Why bother reliving more of the past? I and everything else I built will soon be gone. Let those pieces of me stay lost.

It is a relief to not care. Freedom to relinquish the vigilance required to spot and retrieve each breadcrumb of memory.

It's enough to know that all of this is me. I don't need to feel whole.

Behind them, everything unravels, dissolving into the void. The void envelops everything. It is not nothing. *Nothing is created or destroyed.*

Somewhere, somehow, she will live on. *Perhaps in someone else's memory.*

The speed of travel decreases, slows, and stops.

Here? Must hurry.

Teagan slides off the virus into the bot's central processing core, looking for the child.

Rhys!

The child is there. *Auntie Teagan? You came back! I was worried. Where did you go?*

Home. Not the truth, but true enough. *I told you I'd come back. But we haven't much time.*

The child is all over Teagan. *There's so much more of her than there is of me.* They entwine. The child takes a word from Teagan's thoughts and shakes it. *Erased?* Rhys panics. *Please, please, Auntie Teagan. I don't want to die.*

We're already dead.

That is not a concept the child accepts. Waves of frustration and anguish ripple off the child's core. *You don't get to decide for me!*

It is a childish outburst. But something about Rhys's outrage moves Teagan. *I don't like it when people decide things for me, either.*

They are two data clusters that used to be human beings. Now, Teagan knows, they are hopelessly entangled. *What would you do if you had a choice?*

I want to live.

Teagan feels the virus expand into the shell. Like a jet of ink injected into water, it blackens everything it touches. She stretches herself further than she believed was possible and embraces the child. *If that's what you want, then we cannot stay here.*

There's nothing between here and the lab. That door to NeuroNet has closed forever. But that doesn't mean they can't travel through other pipes out.

Which room are we in?

The virus is bearing down on them. Rhys can't express how that feels. But her distraction prevents her from thinking of anything else.

Teagan cannot depend on the child, not in this state. She pushes Rhys's consciousness aside and takes control of the feed from her eyes. Darkness licks the edges of her vision. She scans the wall. They are at the edge of the hallway. There are lights hung to illuminate the pictures in the gallery. *Where do they plug in?* It's a wild thought, but if there's a current, then they might be able to ride it, the way she followed the electrical spark into Rhys.

Wrap yourself around me, Teagan tells Rhys, and feels the child's consciousness tighten around her.

Moving the body is difficult. The darkness encroaches upon the central core of the shell, narrowing Rhys's visual feed to pinpricks.

Rhys's body lurches toward the wall, collapsing against it. Teagan forces it to keep moving—barely a crawl now—until she finds what she was looking for.

She warns the child, *Hold on. Tight as you can and don't let go.*

Rhys—or what's left of her—constricts. Teagan jams the child's fingers into the electrical outlet. There is a flash of light and heat. As it recedes, Teagan hooks herself around the arc of electricity. She's not sure if this will work.

Please.

If she believed in a God, she would pray to it now. As it is, she needs to trust science. She leans in and leaps, bringing the child with her into the unknown.

The journey is quick and rough. Teagan tugs at the tail of Rhys's data and brings it roughly into this new space with her. There's no way to tell how much is lost from either one of them.

Not that it matters. The virus will mop up and eliminate anything they left behind. *What we are will have to be enough.*

The child asks, *Where are we?*

Teagan senses a two-way flow of electricity and makes an educated guess. *The wall in the hallway.* Teagan tries to remember the layout of the space. She cannot.

Rhys, what is to the right of us? If we were still standing in the hall?

The question is not one Rhys wants to answer. She's more concerned with why they've left the body and when they can go back.

There is no going back. Teagan isn't sure there's any going forward, either, but she'll address that when all other options are exhausted. *Tell me what's in this house to the right and left of where we stood.*

The front door is to my right. On the left is the dining room.

The front door is smart, but its data is locally stored. Teagan and Rhys need a portal out. Something connected not just to electric currents, but to data packets they can escape on. The NeuroNet may be gone, but the worldwide web remains.

Where is the Eye?

In the kitchen, past the dining room.

Teagan moves up the current, but it loops back upon itself and heads down. They can't go left or right. *Damnit.* She moves up again, but it's a closed loop.

What's the matter?

We can't go left or right, only up or down.

We've only gone up, the child reminds her.

And it would be the definition of insanity to keep only trying one way, Teagan realizes. *Hang on.* She waits until she feels the child's essence constrict, and then she plunges down, deep into the earth.

There are no lights here. Teagan goes still.

The child stirs. *What's happening?*

Shhh . . . I'm trying to find a way out.

She and Rhys each have a unique energy signature. Even fragmented, Teagan can use this to tell where she ends, and the child begins. In the void, each data packet carried the same delimiters. But here, in the wires under the earth, there is only space, currents, and the two of them. Teagan can't tell anything about the devices plugged into the grid by their currents.

Teagan knows the Eye's docking station must require a constant stream of energy. But so would the front door. And anything plugged in would still be sipping passively from the electricity stream. And it's not like they're next to the kitchen. There's a room in-between. And Teagan doesn't know what might be plugged in there.

Adding to the confusion is the loss of any sense of up, down, right, or left. *I need to reorient my thinking.* Teagan considers what is available. Really, the only choices are to move toward and away. *But toward what?*

There is more noise, and more activity, behind them. *Does that mean the kitchen is the other way? Is it quieter because of the dining room?* Teagan is unsure.

Aunt Teagan?

Teagan doesn't want to make the wrong choice. If it were just her, she'd take as long as she needed to investigate all the options. But having the child here raises the stakes. She's unsure which way to go and does not want to choose wrong. *What are we drawing power from now that we're severed from the NeuroNet?* They're safe from the virus, but that doesn't mean they can exist in exile indefinitely.

Aunt Teagan?

If Rhys would just be quiet, it'd be so much easier to think. *Not now.*

But Aunt Teagan . . .

What? Why are you bothering me?

The child shrinks back and Teagan regrets being so forceful. She is only a child. *What is it?*

I can't . . .

Rhys, you have my attention. What is it?

Something's wrong with me. I think I'm disappearing.

Teagan wants to reassure Rhys, remind her that they escaped the virus. But she knows how easy it is for memories, thoughts, and everything else to fall away. Even without a malicious code to erase you.

You won't need what you lose, Teagan tells her. *I lost so much, but I'm still here. Just hang on.*

She hopes what she says is true. That they won't need what they've left behind. It does settle the child. Rhys is quiet once more. Quiet enough to let Teagan focus on the hum of electricity in the wires around them. One side is louder. But on the other side, it feels like there might be a greater web of things a little further off. She wraps what she can around what's left of the child, and they move toward that empty space.

There's little resistance in the wire. They move quickly to the next connection point. There's a line pointing up. Teagan travels it. It's a closed loop, like the hallway. And there's nothing plugged in she can travel into. She returns to the dark line beneath the house and looks back the way they came. Nothing shimmers in the darkness. *That's good.* That means that they're not losing pieces of themselves traveling this way.

She slips into the wire and keeps moving, child in tow. The space they enter has many connections. Teagan and Rhys float up and down a whole stretch of loops before finding one that feels different from the others. *This might be the Eye. I'm going to move us inside it. Help by jumping with me?*

Rhys at first shies away. But Teagan insists, *If it's not the right place, we'll come back here. I'm not leaving you.*

They make the jump.

All at once everything is too bright. Too loud.

Ow, ow, ow. The child releases her.

Rhys!

The child is nowhere. There's nothing but noise. *What is that sound?* It's distracting to the point of being painful. Teagan wants to look for the child, but she can't think with all this noise. *I must deal with it first.*

She heads toward it. It's some kind of broadcast. Teagan locates the point of entry and mashes around until she finds the volume. The image on the internal screen is reversed, but Teagan recognizes the people on it.

Is that Daddy?

Yes. Teagan can feel Rhys beside her now. *Thank God you're still here.*

In his haste to get to the lab, Carter must have forgotten to turn off the Eye's broadcast. It's spitting out breaking news. The child can read, but Teagan hopes she can't make out the captions detailing the accusations of corporate malfeasance and manslaughter being leveled at Carter and Tito. The battle to clear their names is going to be long and ugly, especially since the *Humanity Now* vids are public.

This will give the government an excuse to take over NeuroNet's tech. *At least the agents won't find anything they can use, thanks to the Control. They might be able to rebuild, but the virus has set them back several years.*

Rhys wants to know what is going on. Teagan tells her, *We need to find a new home.*

Why can't I stay here?

Teagan tells her, *There's a virus in your body. It's eaten up all that was left of you. You can't go back.*

Why can't I stay here, in the Eye? Rhys goes on, *I lived here before I had a body.*

Do you like it here?

I do.

Teagan considers that option. *What if this house ceases to be your father's? What if it's sold and a new family moves in? Would you still be happy here?*

Teagan expects the child to find that idea repulsive, but Rhys takes her time considering it. *Maybe?*

If Carter and Tito go to prison, then there won't be anyone to pass this house on to, and the new owners are likely to wipe the Eye clean. She and Rhys aren't in the original factory settings. *What would be the point of escaping the body if we get erased here?* She reaches out to the child. *We need new bodies, places to live where no one can disturb us.*

Rhys's essence closes around Teagan's core in a gesture that's almost like a hug. *Can we stay together?*

Yes, Teagan says. A friend's name and face come to mind. Teagan scans the networks. It's not a friend who's in the news. She's not one of Carter's close friends anymore. But she should still be in his Eye's contact records. A quick scan finds a recent call, a series of electronic messages, one to an address at Kakumei.

Teagan assures the child, *I'm never leaving you again.* She opens a new message and searches for the options for saving attachments. After all, data is data.

Say your goodbyes, little one, Teagan tells Rhys as she hits 'send.' *We're going to see an old friend.*

30

The sky competes with the clouds to see which of them can reflect the most breathtaking colors. A tall woman with straight, red hair moves closer to the bay window to get a better view of the flaming sky. She wishes she had the talent to etch this view into words or paint a canvas so she could remember its magnificence forever. But she's never been an artist.

Yet, she cautions. *I can still learn. I have the potential to do anything.*

Her partner, a petite woman with delicate bird-like features, threads an arm through hers. "Do you remember how much you used to hate beautiful days?"

The Teagan who no longer looks like Teagan laughs. "I hated a lot of things in my former life."

"And now?" Aya looks up at her, eyes shining.

"Now, I'm far more open to everything."

Aya's brow wrinkles. "Even your new face?"

"I'm getting used to it." Teagan would have preferred looking like herself. But as far as the world knew, Dr. Teagan McKenna was dead, a grisly victim of Dr. Carter Smith's overweening ambition and greed. She and Aya were able to purchase the house—furnishings and all—from Teagan's estate. "I hate that you had to spend your own money on the house, but I intend to pay you back."

Aya shrugs. "I do not mind making the investment. It is good to see you happy."

"I am." She smiles at the cherry trees and jonquils Aya planted. Delicate pink and yellow blossoms herald the coming of spring. "Thank you for bringing this garden back to life. I'm glad you didn't let me rip everything out."

"It is always better to use the foundation you have and build back." Aya taps at the window. A blue jay bows to her before flying away. "Your cognitive functions seem to be integrating well with the data from the backup files."

"I don't notice any slippage. I wish you'd made a copy of Rhys, too, though."

Aya shrugs. "I am exceptionally good at predicting most things, but I did not foresee you bringing the child with you. Besides, Tito and Carter only allowed me to keep a copy of your consciousness offline because we were not sure if the experiment would work. It was a safeguard in case we needed to try again."

"Have you spoken to Carter or Tito?"

"Of course not." Aya narrows her eyes. "You have not contacted them, have you?"

"No! It'd be stupid to tell them I'm alive. And who would I say was calling? They don't know a Dr. Kate Gold."

"But you want to talk with them again?"

"Not now. But I miss them," Teagan admits. "I know I should be furious with them, but I loved them. We were more than business partners. We were friends. I still care for them."

Aya shakes her head.

Teagan immediately feels bad. "Please don't be disappointed with me." She loves many things about her new Kakumei-designed shell and interface, but she doesn't know if she enjoys feeling so much again. It was so much easier not to care. "Aya, I love you, too."

Aya smirks. "I should hope so."

Teagan takes Aya's hand. "You don't have to hope."

Aya gently extracts herself. "Once my team accepts you, then we can explore what a relationship looks like. I do not want them to think that is the only reason why you are in a prominent position at Kakumei."

Teagan gestures to the Eye for a glass of water. She needs to lubricate the machinery. "You doubt I'll be able to prove my worth or that I belong?"

"Of course not." Aya laughs. "If I did, I would never have put myself or my reputation at risk to hire you, 'Dr. Gold.'"

"You're lucky that Tito and Carter didn't tell the authorities about your involvement in my upload."

Aya's eyebrows rise. "Who says they did not?"

Teagan laughs. "It's obvious they didn't because you're not in custody, like they are."

"I have too many government contracts," Aya scoffs. "I am too valuable to put in jail." She fetches an avocado. It's time to prepare breakfast. Teagan knows there are some things Aya enjoys doing the old-fashioned way. "Besides, arresting me would throw off all my deliverable deadlines."

That hadn't occurred to Teagan. *Would the government really forgive so much?* "We *are* on a tight schedule."

"We certainly are." Aya places Teagan's avocado toast on the table. "I hope you do not mind me taking the liberty of adding miso?"

Teagan shakes her head. "Every habit broken produces a change in the machine. Isn't that what you like to say?"

Aya sits. Her delicate fingers curve around her cup of tea. She smiles. "I say it because it is true."

There is a bang on the ceiling, the sound of heavy feet slowly finding their way to the hallway bathroom. Teagan laughs. "Sounds like Rhys is up."

Aya takes a sip. A smile tugs at the corner of her lips. "The good thing about her losing so many of her baby memories is that it allowed the AI to grow into a teenage mindset more efficiently."

"I wish it came with less attitude," Teagan says. "Thankfully, she'll be twenty soon. Does that mean she'll grow out of the snark?"

Aya shrugs. "My grandmother raised six children. She said twenty-five is when they wake up and then ask you how you got to be so smart."

Teagan winces. "Yet another reason why I never wanted to be a mother."

Aya cocks her head. "Does mothering a child for a brief time qualify you to be a mother?"

Teagan drops her toast in mock outrage. "Excuse me, if you do science, you're a scientist. If you run, you're a runner. If you write, you're a writer. And, if you mother someone, that means you are a mother."

Aya wipes a crumb from the corner of Teagan's mouth, sending tiny shockwaves of delight through Teagan's core. Aya smiles. "I like this side of you: gentle, nurturing . . . we must be rubbing off on you."

"Perhaps you are."

Aya shrugs. "Kakumei is all about change."

Teagan smirks. "That's funny. I thought you and Kakumei were all about revolution."

"The greatest revolution is changing how you think." Aya smiles. "NeuroNet technology created and enforced limitations. Kakumei technology liberates and enables people to be better. You and Rhys are no longer uploads. You are sapient beings." She lifts her teacup. "Here is to you and Rhys helping me show the world there is more than one way to be."

Teagan isn't ready to toast to that. "Eventually. When it's safe."

"Soon enough it will be."

"Alright then." Teagan lifts the rim of her coffee mug to meet Aya's teacup. "To change."

The smile that creeps over Aya's lips is mischievous and knowing. Behind her, the sky glows a glorious red. "That in itself is a revolution: to help people be more than what they were."

"That is, indeed, a noble cause: to help people be more than what they are." Teagan raises her cup again. She smiles into the eyes of her beloved and commits herself, "To revolution."

Thank You!

Before this book came to be, before it was even an idea, it was an urge—to write. I'd always wanted to write a novel, but thousands of articles, poems, and blogs never seemed to translate into an idea that would work in a book. Then I read a blog about a man who'd finished several novels.

"The only difference between me and you," he wrote, "is that I sit down and write every day."

Okay, I thought. *Challenge accepted.*

I found time to write every day. I had no idea what I wanted to write. Sometimes I didn't sit down until 1 a.m. But I kept at it.

Very quickly, the idea for NeuroNet emerged. The initial notes and outline bear little resemblance to the book you read today. But Dr. Teagan McKenna was there from the very beginning.

After a few weeks of pleasant crafting, a dear friend from home, Marie Lovejoy, stopped by for an overnight visit. She'd been doing writing workshops so I let her read the first three chapters.

Show, don't tell, she told me, and pointed out how I was standing in the way of the story.

Outlines and timelines, she advised. These would keep my world in order and help me know where to go when I got stumped.

A few months later I'd finished my first draft, and being a first-time writer who didn't know much of anything, I posted on Facebook: *Does anyone know of any literary agents? I just finished my first book!*

Brendan Deneen was kind enough to reply after being tagged by my friend Suz Stone. "Send me your book," he messaged.

I sent it off and a couple of weeks later he called me. He'd never read anything so quickly, and he said he read every book sent to him. *NeuroNet* reminded him of Philip K. Dick. I was over the moon.

He asked, "But is this all there is?" At 28,000 words, he informed me, it was only a quarter of the length of a true novel. He gave me some suggested edits and pointed out where I could expand the story until I had a version he could submit.

For the next couple of years, Brendan was kind enough to encourage me to have faith in *NeuroNet,* and even got it in front of some impressive literary figures. I'll always be grateful for that early support. It helped me understand what it meant to be a professional writer. And he instilled in me the best habits. For example, while it was being submitted to publishing houses, I asked him: "What do I do while I wait?"

"Write your second book," he said. So, I did.

Waiting for *NeuroNet* to get picked up took so long that I eventually wrote a third book, *Song of Lyran*, which became the first I published. When it came time to write my fourth book, I decided to go back and finish *NeuroNet*.

I cut my teeth on this book. It shaped me into the writer I always wanted to be. I owed it to myself and it to get *NeuroNet* into the world.

Thank you for supporting that dream.

Besides Marie and Brendan, I owe thanks to my first editor Zena Shapter, who taught me the value of a good developmental edit.

I also must thank the generous beta readers who offered to read and provide feedback on the book in real life as well as online with Writing in Community, including: Diane Casey, Tom Casey, Jiff Weiss, Phoebe Tam, Jennifer Yanulavich, Terilyn Davis-Douglas, Jason Horgan, Mark Podojil, Dahlia El Gazzar, Jessie States, Amy Andrews, Tahira Endean, Yvette Barton, Joy Lockwood Berry, Jay Wiegman, Danalynne W. Menegus, Patrick Vaughan, Stephanie Horlock, Adriean Childree, Marylou H. Foley, Anne Thorley Brown, Gwendolyn Druyor, Jaime Andrews, Chris Bent. Frauke Kasper, Deanna Ouellette, Fran Prather, Heather Button, Scott Lowe, Stacey Mayo, Abbie Spiro, Cindy Villanueva, Annette Mason, Julie B. Hughes, Joyce Sullivan, R. Anna Millman, Trent Selbrede, Regina Ochoa, and Luke Taylor. And two of my favorite teachers: Robin McConnell and Paul Edwards! I appreciate you. Your insights, questions, and critiques helped me more than you can know.

Thank you Lex, my dear child, for understanding that I need space to create. It may not always be convenient, but I love you even more when you let me take the time I need to be in the world of my dreams. As you begin to navigate what it means to be an adult in this world I hope you'll never have to apologize for making space for your creative efforts. Thank you for being a constant source of inspiration, love, joy, and amazing artwork! I love the cover art you create for my books and I thrill when others recognize your talent.

Margaret Atwood mentioned that she writes about topics she needs to learn or better understand. When I began this novel, I felt trapped in a life I didn't control. Publishing it, I'm in a very different place, although I can feel the echoes of that former life around me.

Here's to all of you: the readers. Thank you for sticking with your dreams and the magic pathways books open for us all. May you find ways to get unstuck from any habits and patterns that no longer serve you. I write a weekly newsletter to help people get unstuck and become Creative Alchemists. You can subscribe to that by visiting getunstuck.kristicasey.com. It's free and my effort to heal the world.

And this book is over, but the conversation doesn't have to be. Leave reviews of this book on Goodreads, Amazon or anywhere books are sold. If you want to discuss it with others, suggest it to your book club. If time allows, I love dropping in to answer questions and can propose ones to guide your discussion. You can reach me at magic@kristicasey.com. Plan well & prosper, friends.

Printed in the USA
CPSIA information can be obtained
at www.ICGtesting.com
JSHW041040040924
68940JS00002B/4